About Sarah

Sarah lives on the south coast of the UK with her family and works for the NHS.

She has written in a freelance capacity for magazines and business journals and writes scripts collaboratively with two friends which have been performed at arts centres and venues across the south.

'*It started with a shoe*' is the second book in 'The Happy Wanderers' series.

Other books by Sarah

The Postcard in the Window ('The Happy Wanderers' series)

It Started with a Shoe

SARAH SCALLY

First published in Great Britain in 2024

Copyright © 2024 by Sarah Scally

The moral right of Sarah Scally to be identified as the author of this work has been asserted in accordance with the Copyright, Designs and Patents Act, 1988.

All rights reserved. No part of this publication may be reproduced or transmitted in any form or by any means, electronic or mechanical, including photocopy, recording, or any information storage and retrieval system, without permission in writing from both the copyright owner and the publisher.

A CIP catalogue record for this book is available from the British Library.

ISBN: 9798876964984

This book is a work of fiction. Names, characters, businesses, organisations, places, and events are either the product of the author's imagination or used fictitiously. Any resemblance to actual persons, living or dead, events or locales is entirely coincidental.

Dedication

For Chris, my valentine x

Chapter One

PHOEBE WALKED back to her desk and plonked down. The movement woke her computer and the monitor lit up, asking for her password.

"Well?" Penny's head popped up above the desk divider. She widened her eyes expectantly, causing numerous horizontal lines to appear on her forehead. Phoebe looked at the older woman and shook her head.

"Oh love, I'm sorry."

"Me too." Phoebe clamped her scarlet-painted lips together to stop her chin from wobbling. She brushed her blonde curls away from her face, defiant; she wasn't going to give Thomas Johnson the satisfaction of making her cry at work, again!

"Here, you get off," Penny said, her voice upbeat. "Have an early lunch. Tell me about it later when you've…" She flapped her hand, the meaning clear: *when you've calmed down*. Penny didn't *do* tears. She'd been through several traumatic experiences herself and had only returned to work recently after the unexpected death of her husband. Stiff upper lip and keeping busy was how Penny coped. And right now, Phoebe was grateful for it. If she'd been offered sympathy, she'd have collapsed into a sniveling mess. She sniffed.

"You sure?"

"Of course; and if the toss pot comes over, I'll cover for you."

Phoebe laughed, grateful for the attempt to cheer her up.

"Go on." Penny urged, glancing at her watch. "Take the full hour; I'll go at one."

Phoebe grabbed her bag. She didn't need telling twice. "Might not come back."

"Give over, ye daft sod. You'd miss me too much."

Phoebe gave a watery smile and blew her friend a kiss. It was true, she would; but at this moment she'd like nothing more than to walk out of the Planning office and never return.

Outside the 1960s Council building the sun was high. Phoebe stood at the top of the impressive flight of stone steps that led to the Simonton Council offices and hitched up her shoulder bag. Office workers sat on wooden benches dotted around the pristine public gardens. It wasn't a bad place to work; the people were nice, and the pay was alright. She took a deep, steadying breath. It was the second promotion she'd applied for in the last twelve months; the first one being the role now held by her boss, Thomas tosspot Johnson. She didn't know what she'd done to offend him, but there must have been something as it now appeared he'd put the knife in for this latest attempt too. She smoothed down her fifties-style dress, the petticoat coarse against her legs, and breathed in the fresh air. Was it so bad to want… well… more? She was hard working and ambitious. But she was also realistic. She knew that as a single mum to a nine-year-old she needed a job that was flexible too, at least for a few more years. Her stomach rumbled and brought her back to the more pressing issue of food. First stop, lunch. Then she'd find a quiet place to lick her wounds in private. She set off towards Simonton High Street.

A thriving market town, Simonton was all that Phoebe had ever known. It had a good mix of independent shops and chain stores and was big enough to find most of your weekly necessities. Five minutes later, having targeted the Buttery Bap sandwich shop, she stood at the side of the High Street and waited for the traffic lights to turn red. She clutched a brown paper bag; a sandwich nestled inside with a can of tropical drink, a treat to improve her mood. When the lights changed, she stepped out in front of a shiny grey Range Rover. She was two strides across, thinking about where to eat her sandwich, when her back leg caught.

"Ow." She stretched into a full lunge. Her left foot was caught and, shuffling backwards, she inspected her now rather painful ankle. A smile flicked across her lips at the sight of her polka dot shoes—an impulse buy from a local indoor market. She sighed when she spotted the heel, firmly wedged in a manhole cover. She gave it a tug and tried to turn it, but it wouldn't budge. She glanced at the Range Rover, mouthing "sorry" to the couple inside and noticed a pensioner who'd now paused on the pavement, leaning against her tartan shopping trolley. Phoebe wasn't sure if she had stopped to watch the sideshow or to catch her breath, but she felt her cheeks heating up at the attention as she bent to undo the thin ankle strap. She stepped out the shoe, the tarmac warm beneath her bare foot, as a car tooted and made her jump. The lights were now green and the traffic on the other side of the road was beginning to move. Her heartbeat quickened. What was she going to do? It really wasn't sensible to be standing in the middle of the road and, to prove her point, a whiny moped swerved round the Range Rover and accelerated away, missing her by inches. But she couldn't just leave her shoe sticking in the road. The Range Rover's door opened, and a man hopped down. His wife watched his movements with interest.

"You having trouble?" He smiled confidently as he approached. "May I?" He nodded at the shoe.

"Go ahead, it won't budge."

She caught a whiff of his aftershave as he moved past, and Phoebe's eyes glanced over him as he bent down to wiggle the shoe. Chinos and a black cotton shirt, smart in an understated way.

"The heel's wedged."

She started, realizing he was speaking to her.

"If I pull it, you might lose the plastic tip."

More expense. Phoebe sighed. "Still be cheaper than getting a new pair," she replied and pushed a wave of blond hair away from her face. She caught sight of the huge queue now forming behind his vehicle and groaned. "Crikey can this day get any better?" she mumbled, and he glanced up. He paused, shoe in hand, to study her face.

"Are you having a bad one?"

"You could say that."

"Well, only one day until the weekend." He continued to look at her, and she felt heat rising in her cheeks, again. She wasn't used to being studied like that. She glanced away, lifting her hair so the cooler air could get to her neck. He was right; it *was* Friday tomorrow and that meant two whole days at home while Celeste was away camping with her Brownie pack. They were both looking forward to it.

"Er, sorry, I think-" she nodded at the line of vehicles that now snaked through the High Street, "we'd probably better leave it… thanks for trying though."

With a last tug the shoe came away and the man shot backwards. Instinctively, Phoebe grabbed him. His arms were firm beneath his soft shirt and her fingers closed, gripping him. They paused, then abruptly she let go.

"Sorry." A nervous laugh escaped her lips.

"Yours, I believe, Cinders?" He held up the shoe; it was still intact except for a slight scratch on the back. "Perfectly wearable."

"Thank you," she whispered and took it in both hands.

"Will you be alright now?" He took a step forwards, a look of concern on his face.

"Yes. Thank you so much for your help." Neither of them moved. "And no damage either." She turned the shoe over in her hand, grateful

she had somewhere else to focus rather than on him, as an initial butterfly in her stomach grew into a kaleidoscope.

"Do you want to-" he pointed to the side of the road.

"Yes, thank you," she smiled, throwing him a quick glance, before a car horn blasted. She heard him gasp and they both looked up.

"Oh, I'd better…" he pointed to the huge queue of traffic now clogging up the High Street. "I need to…" He waved at his passenger who was scowling through the windscreen.

"Yes, of course. You should go. Thank you. It was lovely to meet you."

"Mike." He held out his hand and she shook it. They smiled at each other; their hands still clasped in midair as they lingered.

"Thanks, Mike," she whispered. The smell of his spicy aftershave floated towards her; she wanted to lean in and inhale deeply, but they released their hands and he backed towards his car.

"Don't forget your lunch." He pointed to the brown bag on the kerb, and she nodded. By the time she'd retrieved it, the vehicle had gone.

Mike glanced for one last time in his rearview mirror, watching the figure in the distinctive fifties-style dress. Like a disorientated Marilyn Monroe, she hobbled back to the pavement and inspected her shoe. She certainly stood out from the crowd; red polka dots will ensure that. Reluctantly, he dragged his eyes away and turned his attention back to the road in front.

"Earth calling Mike. Come in Mike."

He glanced over, to see a glum-looking Heather staring at him.

"Sorry Heather. That poor woman. Good job I got her shoe out. Anyway, you were saying, you've moved out from Amir's?"

She nodded.

"And back in with your mum?"

She nodded again.

"And how is Eddie taking that?"

"It was good at first, I think she liked having me back; but I worry that I'm getting in the way between her and Tolly now."

Mike nodded; Eddie and Tolly's story was a heartwarming one. Two retired people, who had recently been through the mill only to meet when Tolly, an ex-Colonel, had set up a rambling group called The Wanderers. Recovering from a hip operation, he had been reluctant at first, but had persevered to help his grandson prepare for a Duke of Edinburgh expedition. Now, one year on, Eddie and Tolly were still together and flitting between their two homes. It was partly because of the group that Heather and Amir had also met, one year ago, but that was where the similarities ended between Heather and her mum.

"What happened with the two of you? I thought you and Amir were solid." Approaching a roundabout, Mike risked a glance across and noticed how gaunt she looked. He liked Heather, he liked *all* the Wanderers, but he did wonder how Heather and Amir's relationship could have fallen apart so quickly. He pulled out, navigating the traffic then checked himself. He shouldn't ask too many questions; he didn't want to upset Heather and neither did he want the Wanderers to think he was taking sides.

"I think we were both too busy building our businesses. We were tired all the time, and living above the camping shop didn't help," she said with feeling. "He was always thinking about work, and never set any boundaries." She snorted, sadly. "It sounds pathetic when I say it." She turned to gaze out the window. "Maybe I should have cut him some slack," she paused before turning back; Mike could sense her looking at him, as he concentrated on the road ahead.

"It doesn't sound pathetic," he sympathised. "I'm divorced, remember? Pamela and I had those same arguments. I was so focused on work; I would eat and sleep it if I was working on an idea. Businesses demand a lot, particularly at the start. It's like having a new baby, that's what Pamela said… right before she moved out" he added, pulling a face. "I just thought you were love's young dream, that's all."

He glanced over at the sound of Heather's bitter laugh.

"What, don't you think there is such a thing?"

"You're asking the wrong person, Mike."

"Why don't you text him? See if he wants to meet to discuss it all."

She turned sharply, making the seat belt lock. "No way!" She frowned. "He knows where I am."

"But some people aren't very good at backing down. Why don't *you* be the grown up?"

She chewed the inside of her cheek. "I want him to show how much he cares."

"Some sort of grand gesture? Does that really happen, outside of the movies I mean?"

She went back to staring mournfully out the windscreen. "If it doesn't, it should."

An image of the woman with the shoe came into Mike's mind; he was dressed as Prince Charming, shoe in hand, and she was Cinderella. He frowned; he hadn't even got her name. Heather shuffled in the seat next to him and the image popped.

"Anyway," he cleared his throat, "how is your mum? And poor Tolly, I heard about his brother."

Heather sighed. "It's been a sad business about Morris, very unexpected." She glanced across. "Poor Tolly collected his ashes a fortnight ago, but he seems okay. He's even started talking about a motorhome again," she chuckled softly, and Mike slowly shook his head.

"Oh no. He's *still* talking about that. Still comparing the pros and cons to a caravan?"

Heather looked over and laughed. "I think Jack upset him. He was taking the mick out of caravan names—the 'Fleet-foot Conqueror',"

she made air quotes with her fingers, "the 'Royal Ranger'… that sort of thing. Tolly likes one called the 'Swifty 500'." Mike groaned.

"Jack said it should be the 'Snail 500'."

He gripped the steering wheel and chuckled in appreciation; he'd missed their outings over the last few weeks. "As it was Jack," he added, "I'm sure he'll be forgiven. That grandson can do no wrong in his eyes."

"You remember we're going camping this weekend, to scatter Morris's ashes at Gundry's Tower. You coming to join us?"

Mike screwed up his nose. "It feels like it should be a family thing."

"Well, I'm not really family either."

He realised she was right.

"There'll be a few of us. The plan is to walk to the Tower in time for sunrise on Saturday, then have croissants or bacon butties and fizz afterwards. It should be lovely. A real fitting tribute."

It did sound nice, and Mike was always happy for an excuse to reunite with the original members of the Wanderers walking group.

"Go on then," he said as if under sufferance, "I suppose I'll only be working otherwise."

"Great." Heather nodded towards the kerb. "You can drop me here, please. I need to pop into the gallery before I head back to mums." The Range Rover purred to a halt beside the bus stop and Heather jumped down. "Thanks for the lift, Mike," she waved, "see you tomorrow evening."

Chapter Two

Phoebe stepped out through the double doors and onto her handkerchief sized patio. She took a deep breath as she surveyed her garden, her sanctuary. Daffodils would be pushing up along the side of the lawn soon and whilst the garden still looked bare from the winter months, there were signs of hope. Phoebe sighed; unfortunately, she didn't share that feeling at the moment.

The side gate opened with a snap, and she turned to see a little girl hurtling through. She threw herself against Phoebe's hip and the two of them nearly toppled over.

"Celeste!" Phoebe righted herself and rubbed her hip. Her daughter's sticky hands wrapped around her waist and clutched her arms to prevent her from moving.

"Hello darling," she laughed, "how are you?" She stared down at the cherubic face, framed by ringlets, and her spirits couldn't help but lift.

"Agnes says we can watch Enola Holmes-"

"What, again?"

Celeste nodded enthusiastically, her blonde curls bobbing as she moved. Phoebe's were the same, if she didn't rein them in.

"Can we? Can we?" She held her hands tightly together, pleading, and Phoebe chuckled as she brushed the girl's hair away from her hopeful face.

"Have you been drinking pop again?" There was a telltale pink tinge around her daughter's mouth. "You'll have to make sure you clean your teeth properly tonight," she warned, before a scuffling noise by the fence distracted them. Two seconds later her neighbour, Agnes, appeared over

the wooden panel. She stood on the pink plastic step that was kept on her side of the garden specifically for this purpose and held the post to steady herself.

"Hello love." Agnes's tiny, wizened face broke into a smile as she spied her neighbours. "I said, if it was alright with you Phoebe, we could watch that Enid Holmes film again."

The little girl giggled and let go of Phoebe to move towards the fence.

"Enola," she reprimanded. "Not Enid." She jumped up and down, her eyes firmly on the older woman as Agnes flapped her hand and made an unsteady 'W' with her thumbs.

"Whatever, girlfriend," she sneered at Celeste, causing her to giggle again. To Phoebe it was the most beautiful sound in the world, and she gazed at her little girl, who had resumed her jumping. Where did she get her energy from? Phoebe could only dream of it.

"After the week you're having, love," Agnes continued, "I'm happy to hold the fort for an hour or two."

"That's very kind, Agnes, but you don't need to do that. Come round and join us; would you like a glass of wine?"

The older woman shook her head in horror, her weekly shampoo and set not budging an inch due to the layer of hairspray she added as part of her morning routine.

"Oh no, love, no. White wine on my stomach?" It was as if Phoebe had suggested she strip naked and run through town on market day. "Very nice of you. But no. Thank. You! But I know Celeste likes that film, so I will pop round-"

"Luurve that film," Celeste emphasized as the grey curly hair disappeared. They heard Agnes lock her back door and Celeste waited patiently for her partner in crime to stagger round. As she appeared, unsteady in her tartan slippers and clutching a chunky cardigan, Celeste took the older woman's hand.

"Steady on young lady," Agnes laughed. "I'm not as nimble on my pins as I used to be. I wouldn't be able to do the fandango with Bruno Tonioli now, that's for sure." She paused and smiled at the little girl. "1998, now *that* was a magical year."

Celeste watched the older lady's every move. She shepherded her through the patio door and into the cosy living room beyond.

"I've got a homemade lasagna in the fridge," Phoebe said, following them both in. "You'll stop for tea, won't you?"

"Lovely." Agnes held up a gnarled finger, "but only if you've enough."

"You eat like a sparrow," Phoebe laughed, "believe me, I've got enough." Phoebe patted her on the shoulder as she edged past and went into the kitchen. Her relationship with her neighbour was very much one way, with Agnes doing most of the giving. Several times a day Phoebe wondered what she would do if anything ever happened to her—and feeding her a square inch of lasagna was the least she could do for the endless support she provided.

Several hours later, Phoebe walked her neighbour home and waited patiently while Agnes put her key in the back door. She turned round.

"Love, I couldn't say it in front of Celeste but I'm sorry your job didn't come off."

Phoebe waved her hand through the air; she'd almost forgotten about the earlier humiliation.

"You're a smart, independent woman, just you remember that-"

Phoebe snorted, her nose beginning to tickle as she felt the emotion starting to well up.

"There's obviously something better coming your way. In the meantime," Agnes paused and tapped Phoebe on the shoulder, "count your blessings."

Phoebe lifted her eyes and shrugged. "Which are?"

"Why, me and Celeste, obviously. And Zina," she added. "Have you heard from her this week?" Zina was Phoebe's best friend. She'd been seconded to work on a project in Dubai for a whole year and Phoebe missed her like crazy.

"Yes, she knows about the job; she messaged to ask how I'd got on. She's having a great time; working hard, enjoying the sights. It sounds fantastic."

Agnes pushed her door open. She stepped through and turned on the light. As the fluorescent bulbs flicked into action she glanced back. "It'll be alright Phoebe, you're not on your own you know." Now standing in her house, she was on a level with Phoebe; she pulled her in and kissed her on the forehead. "Zina will be back before you know it. Now get back next door, before that little girl finishes cleaning her teeth." She tapped her wristwatch. "That must have been more than two minutes.".

"I'll just wait for you to lock the door."

Agnes tutted, but Phoebe refused to move until her neighbour shut the door and turned the lock inside.

"Sleep tight," Agnes shouted from within.

As Phoebe returned home and shut the front door, she heard Celeste hopping around in the bathroom upstairs. Halfway up the stairs to join her, the landline started to ring; she paused, her hand gripping the banister.

"I'll just get that," she shouted. No response. "I hope you're ready for bed," she added before picking up the phone. "Hello."

"Thank goodness, I thought you might be out. It's Rita." Even down the line Phoebe could hear Rita's trousers rustling as she moved at the other end. Rita Rawlings was a Professor of Plant Evolution. As such, she was normally dressed in weatherproof trousers and jacket which allowed her to sit among vegetation and get close to her subjects. She ran a consultancy business and conducted flora surveys for the Council, which was how Phoebe had got to know her; she was also Brown Owl at Celeste's Brownie group.

"I've got a favour to ask you."

Phoebe's stomach plummeted. "Uh-huh."

"Sylvia has just called; she's come down with some gastro bug… to be honest it sounded awful, and I didn't want to know the details. Anyway, long story short," she took a breath, keen to get to the point in her usual, efficient manner, "she can't make it this weekend. In fact, she doubts that she'll make it out the bathroom this weekend."

"Oh no," Phoebe groaned. "Celeste was *so* looking forward to it." And so was she—two days to tidy up the house and bring some order to the growing chaos. "Do you need help calling the others?"

"What for?"

"To say that you're cancelling."

"That's why I'm phoning you. You used to do expeditions with your parents-"

"Not really expeditions-" They were more like extended holidays touring Europe in a van each summer.

"It'll come back to you," Rita steamrolled over her concern. "Besides, you don't need to do anything; Audrey and I have it under control; we just need to have the right ratio of adults to children."

Phoebe closed her eyes and leant her head back against the wall. Celeste would be devastated if the plans were cancelled. But a weekend away? Camping? It wasn't the quiet two days she'd been planning. A hand on her leg made her jump and she found Celeste gazing up at her with a concerned look on her face.

"Mama, you alright?" She leant her head against Phoebe's hip.

"I'm alright darling, just thinking."

"Phoebe? Are you still there?" Rita's voice boomed out of the receiver.

"Is that Brown Owl?" Celeste stood on tippy toes and cocked her head towards the phone.

"Yes, I'm here," Phoebe put a finger on her lips to shush her daughter. "Celeste was just asking a question."

"So, what do you think? Will you come with us?"

Phoebe closed her eyes momentarily, praying that Celeste hadn't heard. But when she opened them again, the little girl was staring at her, eyes wide with excitement.

"You're coming mama?" Celeste whispered, her hands together in prayer. "Please, please." She held her breath, waiting expectantly.

"I don't know Rita; can I have a few minutes to think about it?"

Rita sighed down the line. "I really need an answer Phoeb, otherwise we *will* have to start phoning round to cancel."

Phoebe glanced down. Celeste's bottom lip stuck out, a frown puckering her otherwise smooth forehead. She'd never be forgiven now if the weekend was cancelled, because of her.

"Okay, I'll help," she sighed. "But you promise, I'm just there for the numbers. I don't want to be put on the spot for anything." She was an excellent wing-woman but hated being the centre of attention; her mind would go blank, and her cheeks would heat up as soon as anyone looked at her.

"I promise. Thank you, Phoebe. See you at the village hall tomorrow, ready to leave at five." As the phone went dead, Celeste let out a squeal.

"Thank you, mama, you're the best! I love you." She jumped up and down, her arms firmly round her mum's waist.

"I love you too, chickpea, but now it really is time for bed. We're going to need all the energy we can muster for this weekend away."

Chapter Three

Phoebe walked towards the wash block carrying a large washing up bowl piled high with smaller dirty ones and cutlery. The Brownies had taken over a field, set away from the main campsite. It was a bit of a trek, having to cross the field and use a cut through in the hedge to get to the main track which looped around the whole site. At the hedge, Phoebe glanced back at their camp; they'd managed to put up the three large bell tents in a type-of circle! The openings faced each other and there was space in the middle for them to sit. Rita's plan was to have a small campfire later, and to gather the girls together for a singsong. They'd discussed the sleeping arrangements already; Phoebe, Rita and Audrey would split between the three tents, with five Brownies assigned to each. Phoebe was already worrying about how to position herself so that if a Brownie tried to leave the tent—or anyone came in—she'd be woken up. The responsibility of looking after other people's children was now becoming obvious and she doubted she'd sleep a wink.

She approached the tidy wash block to find facilities for Men and Women, separated by a long countertop, housing eight stainless steel sink units. Phoebe dropped the bowl gratefully on the side and shook her arms to get feeling back into her muscles. She'd offered to wash up as an excuse to escape for twenty minutes and started to fill one sink with warm soapy water. She started to work through the crockery, washing each methodically as she relaxed into her work. How could such small girls make so much noise? There had been constant screeching all evening and already she had the beginnings of a headache. Rita, sensing the newbie's unease, had assured her that, as soon as dinner was over, the girls would settle down, adding that the hike tomorrow would tire them out. Phoebe chuckled to herself; she had a feeling the only one who'd be tired out tomorrow would be her.

"I didn't realise washing up was so funny."

She jumped, so focused on the rhythmical wiping of each bowl that she hadn't noticed the man arriving at the sink next to her. She turned, then did a double take.

"Oh hello." His eyes widened, equally as surprised. "The shoe lady."

"That's right. Mike?"

His eyebrows rose. "I'm impressed. You remembered."

"Of course; my rescuer." She smiled as they made eye contact and she turned back to the dishes, scrubbing another bowl while she racked her brain for something witty to say.

"How is the shoe?"

"It is fine, thanks to you." She glanced over.

"I'm glad to hear it." He smiled, his eyes a cool, clear blue. He nodded at her pink trainers. "Not brought them on your camping trip then?"

"No," she lifted one foot to show a trainer. "Special occasions only-" she noticed his look of interest. "I'd been for an interview; but they're not sensible for a weekend in the forest."

"Exactly." He laughed and pointed at his own sturdy boots. "So how did the job interview go?"

She groaned and wiped a plate with added force. "I didn't get it."

"I'm sorry," he sympathised, shrugging when she glanced over.

"My gran would say there's something better coming around the corner."

"And did your gran make a habit of walking around corners?"

She laughed and turned back to him. "She was a very clever, lovely woman," she said, pointing a soapy finger in his direction.

"Sounds like her granddaughter."

They locked eyes; the air seemed to still, their attraction obviously mutual.

"Sorry," he cleared his throat, "that was a bit cheesy." He turned back to the sink and busied himself by running the hot water. For a few moments they both continued with their chores, until he caught her eye and nodded towards the pile of crockery on her side. "Looks like you've been feeding the five thousand."

Pleased to be back on a safer topic, Phoebe picked up the tea towel and started to dry them. "I'm with the Brownie group, so I offered to start tidying up." She leant in a bit closer. "Any excuse to get away; I'd forgotten how noisy children can be."

He laughed, his eyes crinkling at the corners. "How did you get roped into that?"

"My daughter is in the group; someone dropped out so-" she opened her arms, resigned to her fate.

"You offered?"

"No, you were right first time; I got roped in! It was either me, or the trip would be cancelled."

"It's really nice to see you again." He glanced at her quickly then straight back to his sink.

"You too, Mike," she smiled, clamping her lips together in case she gave too much away.

"Are you here for the whole weekend?"

"Yes, god help me."

They both laughed and Phoebe felt a spark of something. Attraction? Excitement? She was starting to look forward to the weekend.

"Are you staying here too?" Maybe she'd bump into him again.

He nodded. "I'm here with friends, a type of walking group." He frowned. "I'm not sure what we are exactly, it started out with three of us, then Eddie joined—she's great and she's now together with Tolly," he added quietly. "She keeps him in check. He can be a bit," he looked

around as if expecting someone to be spying on them, "stuffy, I suppose. Now there's quite a few of us; we call ourselves the Wanderers," he grinned, washing a plate slowly. "That's also a bit cheesy, but we're like family now." He paused; his hands submerged in the washing up bowl. He looked sideways at her. "Oh my god, that sounded even cheesier!" They both chuckled, Phoebe shaking her head.

"No, it sounds good."

He nodded. "It is. It's a nice group of people, all ages too." He emptied the water from the bowl and squeezed the cloth. He started to dry the pans and plates, stacking them carefully in the bowl to carry back. He was meticulous, or was he just eking it out to spend more time talking with her? Phoebe frowned, remembering the woman in his car. No, he was just being friendly.

"Well, it was really nice to see you again-" His voice interrupted her thoughts. He was looking at her, waiting.

"Oh, Phoebe."

"Phoebe," he repeated quietly, as if playing with the sound. "That's a nice name."

"Mike!" A sudden movement to the side made them both turn. "There you are. We wondered what on earth had happened to you." A woman appeared, her face flushed, and her shoulder-length hair tied back in a messy ponytail. She glanced over, giving Phoebe a perfunctory grin and she recognized the woman from the car; his wife, she assumed.

"We're waiting to do pudding; Eddie's brought a Lemon Meringue."

"Oh no, more washing up." Mike winked at Phoebe, and she couldn't help but giggle. Po-faced, the woman started to head back.

"Are you coming or not?" She beckoned him impatiently before going around the corner.

"Better do as I'm told." He gave a regretful shrug and picked up his bowl. "Maybe see you back here at some point over the weekend?"

"I'll probably be here after breakfast, lunch and dinner if the girls stay so loud," she sighed and, as he disappeared with a brief wave, she reminded herself not to flirt with a married man.

Chapter four

It felt like the middle of the night as Mike emerged from his tent. He adjusted the beam of his head torch so that it shone on the floor and not in people's eyes and, although still pitch black, he could make out Tolly's outline, standing over by the cars. A small group of people were gathered around him, ready for the walk to Gundry's Tower. Mike zipped up his tent, then his jacket. Shivering against the chill in the air, he plodded over to join them.

"Morning," he whispered, as he joined the group and several faces turned towards him. Heather nudged him with her elbow.

"You may as well turn that off until we get moving," she said, "save your battery."

Mike frowned at her bossiness but did as instructed. On the other side of the car park Amir hovered with Tolly's family; his son, James, daughter in law, Diana and grandson, Jack. They hadn't camped over but had driven up this morning to join the group in scattering Morris's ashes. Standing next to Mike, Heather seemed to be making a point of looking anywhere *but* towards Amir. Mike felt his stomach sink. How was this going to play out if they weren't speaking to each other? Eddie appeared next to him and switched her torch to a low beam.

"Right, everyone here?" Eddie whispered, conducting a quick headcount. "You've got the urn?" She looked at Tolly who nodded, his face sombre. Mike patted his rucksack. He and Jack were charged with everything needed to make bacon sandwiches later; Amir had pastries and was carrying two bottles of fizz and plastic glasses.

"Let's get the show on the road then." Eddie gave Tolly's arm a reassuring rub. "You alright love?" A weak smile flicked across his face, and he bent to kiss her cheek. He held out his tin of mints and waited patiently while those who wanted, helped themselves. The regular Wanderers took a mint; it was now a ritual.

"Thanks for organizing this, Eddie," he said quietly, putting the lid back on the tin. "It's a lovely way to send Morris off on his next journey; Gundry's Tower meant so much to him—to us—as children." He pocketed the tin. "It's got memories for a lot of us, hasn't it?"

Heather agreed. "It has for us too, hasn't it mum?"

Eddie agreed. The Wanderers started to walk away from the campsite, their feet moving quietly across the field, the grass damp with morning dew. They headed towards the footpath. No one spoke. It felt too early to be sociable and, if they were anything like Mike, they were still in the zone between asleep and awake. They were also now aware of the Brownie pack staying at the campsite, following Mike's meeting with Phoebe, and they didn't want to be responsible for waking the little ones this early in the morning.

After a few minutes, they joined the coastal path and the sound of boots hitting the gravel made a satisfying crunch after the quiet tramping on the grass. The dynamics of the group members altered, as they paired up and walked two abreast. The width of the footpath forced them together and as Amir and Jack took the lead, Mike found himself a back marker with Eddie.

"How is Tolly?" Mike whispered, walking close enough that their arms occasionally nudged each other.

"He's alright," she whispered, glancing ahead. "It was such a shock for everyone; there was no warning." She shook her head sadly recalling the awful phone call from the hospital. "With Morris having no family of his own, Tolly has been sorting everything out. His flat took a while to organise; it's been redecorated too, so we've had a very busy few weeks.

This," she nodded towards the rucksack on Tolly's back, which contained Morris's ashes, "will be good for him. It will bring some closure." She patted Mike's arm. "I hope by seeing everyone again he'll be encouraged out of his fog… get him out into the world again."

Mike nodded. Tolly had been noticeably absent from their last couple of walks, and he for one had missed him. As an original member of the group, having founded it with Jack, Tolly brought an air of calm. He engendered the respect and discipline that only a retired Colonel from the British Army could, and made people feel safe, as if everything was under control which (judging by some of their earlier escapades) was no mean feat. No matter how hard Mike tried, he couldn't match the level of authority that Tolly had over the group and they needed him back.

"I don't remember it being this far," Heather mumbled from her position next to Mike; somewhere along the path she'd swapped with Eddie.

"Patience is a virtue." Her mum waggled a finger over her shoulder at Heather and Mike noticed she clenched her jaw as she glared back. Heather's years of being an independent female, with a successful career in Dubai and London, obviously meant nothing to her mum now that Heather was back living under her roof. Eddie had already given her several orders, and they were only thirty minutes into their walk.

Eddie stopped abruptly and frowned.

"Oh."

The line of walkers came to a halt behind her, all gawping at the high metal fencing which now blocked the route. "You used to be able to walk straight along here." Eddie turned three hundred and sixty degrees, her brow furrowing. "Maybe I've got it wrong." They spread out along the fencing and peered through.

"Hey, isn't that where I proposed to you, Diana?" Tolly's son, James, pointed through the fence to a hedgerow which sloped down towards the sea. A couple of inches shorter than his father, they were otherwise very similar in their upright stature. Diana joined him and squinted into the distance.

"I *did*, just by that hedge. We were sheltering from the wind; it was a freezing southwesterly, but Diana was determined to finish a picture."

"It was very romantic," she added, "I'd found some tiny flowers and was sketching them onto a notepad, do you remember?" She looked lovingly at her husband. "Personally, I think it was the wine we'd had with our picnic. We'd got a lift… from Uncle Morris actually." Her smile dropped, bringing them all back to the reason they were here. "It was a lovely day," she gave her nose a rub. "Uncle Morris was over the moon, bless him. We picked up fish and chips to celebrate, back at the house with you…and Thea." She lowered her voice slightly at the mention of Tolly's ex-wife. "Do you remember?"

Tolly nodded wistfully. "I do. We stayed in the garden talking around a bonfire." A silence fell on the group, allowing the family to reminisce. Then, shaking himself free from the memories, Tolly also stuck his hand through the fence and pointed. They followed his finger to where, not far in front of the hedge, was the tip of a white tower. "There it is." His hand dropped to his side and he tutted. "It's so frustrating that we can't just walk through."

Wondering what was going on, Mike looked along the metal barricade and spotted a large truck parked to the side. A man was inside the cab, the engine off, and he appeared to be reading a book.

"Let's ask him."

"Carpenter Construction?" Tolly squinted at the truck's logo. "Why would they be here?" He shook the fencing; it rattled but stood firm.

"Hey!" They'd been spotted and the man jumped out his truck. "Can I help you?" He walked towards them; he was well over six-foot-tall and appeared to be solid muscle. Undaunted, Mike went to meet him.

"What's going on here?" he asked quite reasonably. "We're trying to get to Gundry's Tower."

Unshaven, the rough dark stubble on his chin suggested that the man might have been in the truck all night. He wore a chunky, navy-blue jumper; a badge on his chest announced 'Security' in white, block capitals.

"You can't get this way anymore, mate."

Mike glanced at Tolly; he knew him well enough to know he'd be bristling at this level of informality.

"You need to go back along the footpath and pick up the diversion signs. They're about a kilometre that way. Then you need to turn inland."

"I didn't notice any signs." Tolly puffed out his chest in protest. "Is this a formal closure of the right of way?"

The security guard mirrored Tolly's body language. "They've re-routed the path. You need to go back, and pick up the diversion signs," he repeated. He must have been on a 'dealing with troublesome customers' course and was now putting the theory into practice. His face remained neutral, with no flicker of any friendliness.

"I didn't see anything either." Eddie appeared behind them and looked up at the guard, who now crossed his arms over his barrel-like chest.

"Can't you just let us through to get to the Tower? We'll only be thirty minutes."

The man shook his head, legs shoulder-width apart, standing his ground. Heather nudged her mum.

"Come on. We'd better go back."

The security guard nodded; his face relaxing a tiny amount at the fact that one of them was being sensible. But he didn't move. He remained standing, legs apart, behind the fence. Mike took charge.

"Come on guys. Let's see if we can find another place to stop. I don't think we'll make it to Gundry's in time for sunrise now anyway." He pointed out to sea, to the horizon, where a faint orange glow announced the imminent arrival of the sun. Dejected, they turned around and trudged back, covering the way they'd just come. Mike waited for them all to pass. After a few minutes he followed, then turned around. The security man was still watching, only now he was talking into a mobile phone. He lifted his chin at Mike, giving him a steely gaze while listening to someone on the other end. Mike narrowed his eyes and took a deep breath. The man was only doing his job, but he didn't need to be so rude about it.

"Come on Mike," Heather said quietly next to him, "don't rise to it." She gave his arm a gentle tug then moved off after the others, leaving him to stare at the signage. The fencing was robust and high. It seemed a bit over-the-top for a footpath; obviously someone was trying to keep people away.

"What do you think is going on?" Mike pondered aloud, but when he turned, the others were ahead. Now they'd have to scout for a different spot for breakfast and for Tolly to scatter Morris's ashes. He'd been adamant that it had to be at Gundry's Tower though, so would anywhere else do for Morris? Mike doubted it.

The smell of bacon wafted through the air as the friends charged their plastic glasses with champagne and stood to watch the sunrise.

"Isn't it beautiful?" Eddie cradled her beaker and Amir, eating a croissant, looked out to sea as the colours changed around them. They all fell silent as the dark, grey outlines became lighter and distinct. The orange glow on the horizon lifted, turning first amber then yellow, as the

sun rose into the sky. It was beautiful to watch and for a few moments no one spoke.

"To Morris," Tolly proposed, and everyone joined in.

"To Morris."

"He'd have loved this, wouldn't he?" A murmur ran around the group as they held out their glasses.

"Are you sure you don't want to let him go here?" Eddie asked quietly, but Tolly shook his head.

"No, it doesn't feel right. We wanted to be at Gundry's, and I'll wait until we know what's going on. He can stay with us a bit longer, can't he?"

Eddie nodded. "Of course he can. There's no rush."

She glanced towards the urn; it sat on the grass near their backpacks. Amir caught her eye as he chewed. She shrugged. He knew she'd been hoping that today would mark the turning of a new chapter for Tolly, but it looked like circumstances were conspiring against them. A clatter from behind broke into his thoughts; Mike was holding up a pan full of sizzling, browned bacon.

"Nearly ready, everyone" he shouted, completely oblivious to the moment of reflection going on behind. "Grab a plate, some bread and I'll dish out the rashers." The question of Morris's ashes was forgotten, at least for now, in their scramble to get some breakfast.

Chapter five

Phoebe was enjoying herself. She hadn't expected to, but the girls' happy singing, mixed with the fresh air and superb views, meant she walked with a spring in her step, as she brought up the rear of the Brownie pack. For an hour, they'd been hopping and skipping. They'd stopped twice and had been gathered in for Brown Owl to point out some pretty coast-path flowers—Phoebe had already forgotten the names—and moss growing on the side of a row of trees.

"Some people think that moss hurts the tree," Rita looked at the girls around her. "Do you think that's true?"

"It's true." Jemima was a pale, slight girl who had already come to Phoebe's attention because of her tendency to boss people around. She was the same with everyone, regardless of whether they were a child or an adult, and last night, she'd instructed Phoebe where to put the clean bowls once she'd returned to camp. Jemima was probably trying to be helpful, but the words that had been used were "Hey! Put those bowls in that cupboard." Worse, Phoebe cringed, was that she had done as she'd been told. A seasoned people pleaser, Phoebe decided she could learn a thing or two from Jemima this weekend.

"Well," Rita picked up on Jemima's certainty, "you'd think it would, wouldn't you?"

Jemima nodded, enjoying the attention.

"But actually, moss doesn't harm a tree. In fact, they are an important part of biodiversity. Do you remember girls, we had a lesson on that?" The girls, and Phoebe, nodded; they were going to learn a lot from Rita

this weekend, given her expert knowledge on plants. You didn't become a professor without knowing a thing or two.

They continued along the coast path; Celeste walked alongside her friend Alice, just in front of the back marker, Phoebe. Celeste threw the occasional glance over her shoulder, to check her mum was still there, and Phoebe felt her heart swell. She hadn't realised it would mean so much to her, to have her mum tagging along. An air of calm settled on Phoebe; she should do this more often. Her thoughts were cut short when the group stopped. There were raised voices ahead and she herded the girls to a safe spot, to the side of the coastal path. They bunched up together while they waited patiently for Rita to appear. Behind her was a trail of hikers and Phoebe's heart gave a tiny kick against her ribcage when she recognized Mike. Seeing her too, he waved and strolled over.

"Hi Mike," she smiled, "what's going on?"

Mike pointed to where the Brownies were heading. "The path's blocked off further along. Apparently, we should have followed the diversion signs, but we didn't see any. Did you?"

Phoebe shook her head. "Is it blocked off to Gundry's Tower? That's where we're heading."

"Yes 'fraid so. We were due to go there this morning, early, but couldn't get through this way. It's all a bit of a mix up, so we're heading back." He pointed to the rest of the group who had gathered round Rita to talk. "A few of the Wanderers; Tolly, Eddie," he pointed as he said their names, "that's Heather." Phoebe recognized his wife. "Diana, James, Jack—Tolly's family, and Amir." Some of them gave a quick wave as they heard their names; Heather stood to one side with a sullen expression on her face.

"Nice to meet everyone," she smiled at Eddie. "I'm Phoebe, this is my daughter Celeste… and fourteen other Brownies," she laughed. She looked around. It looked like they'd stopped talking at the front and the girls were hopping around on the grass, getting impatient.

"Well, nice to see you again Mike. Er, I'd better see what Rita wants to do; I mean, Brown Owl," she corrected, glancing to see whether any of the girls had heard. "Enjoy the rest of your day."

"Yes," he smiled. "You too, Phoebe." He lowered his voice, "maybe see you at the sink later?"

She gave a tiny nod and tucked a curl behind her ear, as a tiny fizz of electricity zinged through her body.

Chapter Six

Phoebe sat on a fallen tree trunk and cradled her mug of tea.

"Celeste, watch where you're going sweetheart," she called, as Rita sank down beside her.

"I need this." Rita blew on her drink then sipped it tentatively. Audrey was taking the second watch of the girls who, now that they'd munched through their packed lunches, were getting a second wind and becoming louder. Rita had organized a game of tag to keep them busy while the adults had a breather.

"It's beautiful in here, isn't it?" Phoebe looked up to the treetops. "Lovely and peaceful… well, it would be if it wasn't for fifteen shrieking girls!" She caught Rita's eye and smiled. "They are having a wonderful time, aren't they?"

Rita's face was serene. "Just think, they're getting exercise, fresh air-"

"-and learning loads from you too," Phoebe chipped in. "Volunteers like you are so undervalued." This weekend was really opening her eyes to the work and preparation that Rita had poured into making it possible. "You are a star, you know that?"

Rita shrugged. "I just want to pass on the joy of being out in nature."

"You should join that Wandering group we met earlier. Mike said they go out most weekends."

"Oh, I've already been out with them—just a couple of times," she added as Phoebe eyed her over the rim of her mug.

"I didn't realise you knew them. They all seem friendly, although" she lowered her voice, "Mike's partner doesn't seem to be enjoying herself."

30

Rita paused. She turned to Phoebe; confusion written on her face. "Pamela? I didn't see her. Anyway, she's his ex-wife now."

"I thought she was called Heather?"

"Oh," the confusion lifted, "she's not his wife," Rita laughed. "She is Amir's partner, the tall good-looking guy with the quiffed hair. You know he's Sadiq's son, right? He runs the camping shop in town."

Phoebe squinted, unsure; she was working hard to keep up. She knew Sadiq, Rita's boyfriend; they'd met a couple of times recently. Rita had met him at a weight loss club last year, but she hadn't realised that Amir was his son.

"Anyway, she *was* Amir's partner," Rita lowered her voice. "They've just split up apparently; a real shame."

"She was bossing Mike around like they were a married couple," Phoebe paused; she could trust Rita to be frank with her, "So, is he seeing anyone?"

"Mike? No." She side-eyed Phoebe then turned back to watch the girls. "He divorced a few years ago, Pamela; I never met her. I don't think they were married long, and it all seemed amicable."

"Interesting."

Rita turned, narrowing her eyes at Phoebe. "Why are you so interested anyway?"

Phoebe reminded her about her shoe-rescuing knight in shining armour…well, shiny Range Rover.

"*That* was Mike?" The penny suddenly dropped. "*He* was the one who helped you?"

"Uh-huh." Phoebe raised her eyebrows then looked away, feeling heat rise in her cheeks.

"I see. Now that *is* interesting," Rita nudged her with her elbow. "Do I detect a hint of attraction?"

Phoebe smiled coyly, she shrugged. "He seems nice. But I thought he was married so…" she let the sentence hang. What would she have done if she'd known he was single? Probably nothing. She was so out of practice on the dating scene; it had just been her and Celeste for years, they'd not needed anyone else. She found herself wondering what Celeste might think about him, her thoughts interrupted when a gaggle of laughing girls ran in front of them and flopped down on the floor, gasping for breath.

"This is good." Rita said loudly, getting up and walking over to them. "You're all going to be too tired tonight to toast those marshmallows. Phoebe, Audrey and I will have to keep them all to ourselves." As if to prove they still have plenty of energy, the girls hopped up. One began to chant 'we want marshmallows, we want marshmallows' and within seconds the others joined in, marching in a circle around Rita. One after the other they paraded back into the woods, and Phoebe could still hear the song about marshmallows long after they'd disappeared from view.

Chapter Seven

"Right girls, I've only got a few flumps left, so line up nicely." Phoebe glanced over to the line of Brownies eagerly queueing to grab a marshmallow for toasting on the fire. Phoebe sat on a camp chair next to it. Her job was to make sure the fire didn't spread beyond the circle of stones they'd gathered earlier, specifically for this occasion. She stared into the flames and felt her shoulders relax. She was unaware of the altercation happening further down the line, until a shout caught her attention.

"Girls," Rita's voice boomed out. "What's happening here?"

Phoebe looked across; now in the middle of a small group of them, Rita was holding Celeste's arm. Watching, but deciding it was better not to show any favouritism, Phoebe remained sitting.

"She pushed in, Brown Owl." Celeste nudged Jemima roughly with her elbow.

"Ow," Jemima whined in her high-pitched voice. She shoved Celeste back who staggered, treading on another girl's foot.

"Ow!"

Jemima was holding a marshmallow skewered on a stick. Celeste kept trying to grab it but each time, being taller, Jemima whipped it out of her reach. Phoebe frowned. She got up and walked over.

"Mama, she's already had one and she's pushed in to get another." Celeste pointed to the treat. "That should be mine. I've not had one yet."

"You'll get one in a minute if you behave yourself and queue nicely." Phoebe watched as Celeste's face fell, realizing she wasn't going to get any special treatment from her mum.

"I'm afraid, that's the last one." Rita turned to Jemima. "Have you had one already?"

Jemima's mouth was set firm; she nodded stubbornly. "But so have loads of others."

"In that case you should give that one to Celeste, it's only fair." As Rita was talking Jemima smirked and took a nibble of the marshmallow.

"Jemima!" Rita growled and Phoebe gasped at the girl's audacity.

"Oi," Celeste shouted, "that's not fair." She lifted her foot and kicked Jemima's leg.

"Celeste. Stop that right now." Phoebe grabbed her daughter's arm to make her stop. She could see that Jemima was winding her daughter up but there was no excuse for violence. "Brown Owl, if it's okay with you I think we'd better separate these two. I think Celeste should come and sit with me by the fire."

Rita nodded, grateful for the suggestion to stop them from warring.

"What about my marshmallow?" Celeste whined, but Phoebe turned to glare at her.

"Jemima can keep that one, as an apology for kicking her."

"But she started it," Celeste was on the verge of tears. "It wasn't my fault." Phoebe took Celeste's hand and pulled her away to sit beside her on a camping chair. Celeste burst into tears and Phoebe's heart melted.

"I'm sorry Celeste. You should have had a marshmallow and that was very naughty of Jemima. But you shouldn't have kicked her."

"I was only sticking up for myself. She's a greedy pig-"

"Celeste!"

"She is, and now she's got away with it. I hate her."

Phoebe was shocked by this outpouring and leaned in towards her daughter. She spoke quietly.

"Sometimes you have to let it go, Celeste."

"But why?"

"To keep the peace."

"But that's stupid. She was wrong. Now she's had two and I've had none."

Phoebe stroked her hair, realizing how different they were. She would *never* have stood her ground like that, in fact she still didn't. She always preferred to shy away from any confrontation and keep a low profile. She squeezed Celeste's tiny hand, "how about you have a biscuit now and tomorrow we'll get marshmallows on the way home?"

Celeste sniffed, her bottom lip still sticking out.

"We could melt some chocolate and dip them in that instead of toasting them?"

Celeste gave a watery smile. "Promise?"

"Promise darling. And in the meantime, you keep away from Jemima."

"Okay mama."

Chapter Eight

The alarm clock rang and Phoebe smacked it with a groan. She normally had a sixth sense that woke her a minute before the alarm went off. This morning, however, that sense had been smothered by exhaustion following the weekend. She stretched out, then immediately curled back under the covers. It couldn't be Monday morning already, it just couldn't. But it was! She needed to get up and get moving.

Thirty minutes later she waited by the front door.

"Come on, Celeste," she shouted up the stairs. It had the desired effect as her daughter came barreling down, jumped to a stop on the final step and hastily pulled on her shoes. Phoebe herded her out the door, grabbing backpacks and her handbag on the way. They walked down the path to their trusty but rusty Fiesta, parked on the road outside. She strapped Celeste in, then turned the ignition. Nothing. Phoebe sighed and closed her eyes. Not today. Not now they were already late. She tried again. It hiccupped but didn't fire.

"Sit still, I won't be a min." She hopped out and leant on the front wing. She bounced it up and down, her daughter watching with delight from the front seat as she bobbed in time with it. Phoebe climbed back in, turned the ignition et voila. It worked! The bounce had loosened the starter motor which in turn fired the engine… or something like that. She wasn't an expert, but YouTube had suggested this as a short-term fix. The problem was it was happening more and more frequently, and she really needed to get it checked out. She made a mental note to put it on her To Do list, then glanced back at the house. A movement to the right caught her eye and she spied Agnes watching from the window.

"There's Agnes, look."

Celeste turned and they waved to their neighbour. "We'll pop over and see her tonight."

Celeste nodded her agreement; she was always happy for an excuse to see their neighbour.

"Right kiddo, let's go."

The morning whizzed past in a blur and at eleven o'clock Phoebe stood and peered over the desk divider.

"Penny?"

Her colleague looked up.

"Coffee?"

"Oh yes please. I'll come with you, stretch my legs." Together they walked down the corridor and into the corner kitchen.

"So how did your weekend go? Obviously tiring, as I saw you yawning earlier." She laughed as Phoebe closed her eyes and started to snore.

"Unbelievably shattered this morning. The alarm woke me for the first time in… years. But the weekend was great." Phoebe couldn't prevent the grin from breaking out across her face. "I really enjoyed it. I've told Rita I'd be happy to help again." She watched as Penny spooned instant coffee into two mugs and filled them with boiled water. "Celeste loved me being there, although," she tutted, "we couldn't do what Rita had planned for the girls-"

"Oh?"

"The footpath at Gundry's was closed. There was a diversion in place."

"Oh?" Penny glanced across; her curiosity piqued.

"I wondered if you knew what's happening there. Have you heard anything?"

Penny shook her head then thought for a moment. "Hold on. There was an application for planning permission a while ago. The last I heard was that it was being appealed, so it was put on hold."

Phoebe raised her eyebrows, her faith in Penny remained intact. She knew she'd be up to date with anything going on.

"Have a look in the filing store, there might be paperwork in there, if you're interested?"

Returning to her desk, Phoebe spotted a text on her phone. She smiled, noticing George's name on screen. George was Zina's cousin—Zina had been her best friend since primary school—and one of the many things she missed about Zina working away in Dubai, was the lack of contact with her family and friends. Some of them, like George, she'd also known since childhood. She opened the text expectantly and sipped her coffee as she read it. She gulped, almost spilling the liquid down her front. He was trying to find out information about Gundry's Tower, of all the coincidences, and when she replied to explain as such, they quickly agreed to meet for a catch up at lunch.

On her way out, an hour later, she paused beside the filing store as an image of the Tower came to mind. The store was more of a small closet; lined with rows of lockable filing cabinets. It was where current working documents were held, before being crated up and sent to Archives once the project was complete. She pushed the door; it opened with a loud creak, and she glanced furtively down the corridor. She half expected the complaining hinges to have brought people out but there was no one around. She went in; five minutes wouldn't hurt. The cabinets were arranged in alphabetical order—her boss not keen to progress on the digitisation of records for their office—and quickly she found G-J. She turned the silver key and opened the metal door. She ran her finger along the shelves; Gale, Gallimore—she skipped along a few rows—Gibbon, Gratton, Gulliford. She paused. The next file was Guycliffe, referring to a local project to renovate a crumbling manor house. She backtracked. There was definitely no folder for Gundry. She sighed; this was proving to be more difficult than she'd imagined. The creak of the door made her turn and her stomach plummeted as her boss walked in. Thomas Johnson jerked to a stop by the door.

"Fiona-" He looked equally as surprised to see her.

"Actually, it's Phoebe," she corrected, her neck prickling with irritation. He *never* got her name right. The room was too small for her to get out without brushing uncomfortably past him and, recognising this, he stepped back towards the door.

"If you've nearly finished, I'll wait outside."

She nodded. "I can't find what I was looking for anyway."

"Oh?" He paused; his attention piqued.

"I was just being curious," she mumbled. She'd started the conversation now. "Um, I was trying to find information about Gundry's Tower."

He slowly turned back to face her and allowed the door to close behind them. He took a step closer.

"And why are you interested in Gundry's Tower?"

She swallowed; the air stilled. She ran her finger along a shelf. "The footpath was closed when I was there at the weekend. I just wondered why." She cleared her throat and waited for his reaction.

"Work is happening up there; construction of a new annex to allow for warden assisted living. It's all finalised," he waved a hand with an air of authority. "The paperwork must be in Archives by now. I guess the footpath's closed in the interests of public safety while the work takes place."

She frowned. "I didn't know about that."

"Do you expect to hear about *all* the developments happening in this county?" His tone was prickly, and he narrowed his eyes at her. Although they were roughly the same age, Phoebe had a flashback to being told off by a teacher for failing to complete a homework assignment.

"No," she said quietly, "I suppose not." She looked at the carpet's coarse brown threads, industrial and worn out from the regular footfall of employees.

"Well then," he sniffed, "things are happening all the time. You can't be expected to know everything, can you? Now," he opened the creaking door again and stepped back, "if you'll excuse me, I do need a folder to prepare for a meeting."

"Yes, of course." She hurried out and flashed him a quick smile. She walked along the corridor, expecting to hear the hinges complain as the door closed again. She glanced over her shoulder; he was still staring after her, his face set tight. She straightened her back, trying to fake some confidence, but instead she shivered as a cold shudder ran down her spine.

Chapter Nine

Mike picked up his pint from the bar and went to settle in a corner of the Woodpecker Inn. He was grateful to George for arranging this meeting; he didn't say how he knew this person in the Council, but they'd offered to have a quick chat this lunch time. Mike took a sip of his pint and surveyed the room. Arranged for dining, the place was empty, except for a couple of pensioners at the bar each cradling a half pint. Mike took another sip of his beer. It wasn't bad and he tried to relax against the hard wooden chair. He glanced at his watch, five past twelve already. He hoped this woman hadn't forgotten. Back at the office he had a mountain of paperwork to get through and he didn't really have time for this, but Gundry's Tower intrigued him. He sighed, blowing out his cheeks. He'd just put his glass on the table when the door opened and in walked a woman. It was a good job he'd put his drink on a firm surface otherwise he might have dropped it. It was *her*. Phoebe! She walked to the bar and glanced around. She spotted him and did a double take.

"You again?"

He left the table and walked over.

"I don't suppose—are you George's friend from the Council?"

She nodded. "I should have realised; are you the 'M' in M. Costello designs, George's boss?" She looked him up and down.

"The very same." Mike couldn't stop smiling as he held his hand out and took hers. Her skin was so soft, her hand tiny in his. He lingered, wanting to keep hold of her, but realising that might be a bit weird, he shook it a couple of times then let go. "Can I get you a drink?"

"I should buy you one, for helping me with my shoe."

Mike wouldn't hear of it. "No, let me-"

The barman cleared his throat, bored by their debate, and Phoebe held her hands up in surrender.

"An orange juice and lemonade then, please."

Settled back at the table Mike couldn't believe his luck. He handed the drink to Phoebe and took a sip of his own, to steady his nerves.

"So how do you know George?"

"My best friend Zina is his cousin," she took a drink. "I've known him since we were kids; Zina's working in Dubai at the moment, on some fancy project."

He watched as she paused and pushed a blonde curl away from her face. Her polka dot blouse made him think of her shoe trapped by the manhole cover; was that only last week? He felt like he'd known her for ages.

"So," her voice interrupted, a smile playing on her lips. "George said something about a right of way, and I'm assuming it's Gundry's Tower?"

He nodded.

"I tried to find out something earlier, but I was told that permission has been approved for an annex to be built up there, for assisted living apartments." She shrugged. "Probably an extension to the care home that's already there."

"Can they block the right of way like that?"

"They can apply to close or divert it. The authorities would have to be notified but that's easy to check."

"How do you do that?"

"The Council has to keep the definitive map updated with any changes."

He watched as she tapped her chin, his attention wandering to her red-painted lips. Even at the weekend he'd noticed she was never without lipstick. He liked it, it reminded him of the old cinema starlets.

"I know someone who can check that for me-"

He tuned back in. The footpath.

"I don't want to get you in trouble."

"It's fine," she assured him. "It's a matter of public record, so shouldn't be difficult to find out."

"Great, thank you."

"No problem." She sipped at her drink, looking around the bar. "It's quiet in here."

"Certainly quieter than your weekend," he smiled. "How was the rest of your camp?"

"It was fab," she beamed, revealing pearly white teeth. "I really enjoyed it once I'd learnt to block out the noise." She laughed. "I should be used to it, having a nine-year-old myself but somehow you forget. And anyway, it's normally just the two of us—and Agnes from next door sometimes comes over—so we're fairly quiet at home."

His curiosity was aroused, and he glanced at her hands. His heart skipped; she wasn't wearing a ring. The tinkle of her laugh made him look up and he saw that she was watching him. Her eyes narrowed.

"I'm not married, Mike. Celeste's dad and I aren't together." She licked her lips. "We're still in touch," she added hastily, "and he helps out when he can."

"I'm single too, just in case…" heat prickled his neck. God, he was so out of practice—not that he was ever that proficient!

"I know," she smiled and instantly he felt better. "I thought you were married to Heather initially, but Rita put me right."

"Did she?" He looked at her, waiting for her to go on.

"What?"

He paused with his beer glass halfway to his lips. "Did she tell you all about my good deeds, how I'm a model citizen with amazing conversational skills and a constant stream of jokes which have the Wanderers in stitches?"

Phoebe shook her head, her face deadpan.

"Oh."

She laughed. "We didn't really talk about you."

Well, that burst his bubble. Phoebe must have seen his face fall as she added, "Only because Rita spent more time talking about Heather and Amir, and what a shame it was that they'd split up."

He nodded. "It *is* a shame," he agreed, "although I wouldn't be surprised if they get back together, at some point. They just need to work things through."

Phoebe finished her drink and glanced at her watch. "I'm sorry Mike, but I need to head back to work."

"Are you having a better week?"

Phoebe paused.

"Last week, you were wondering what else could go wrong."

Her face fell as she recalled their first encounter. "Oh, that…the promotion-" She lifted one shoulder. "With being away all weekend, I didn't even think about it."

"The therapeutic outdoors."

She grabbed her tote bag and swung it over her shoulder. "If I find out anything I'll let George know."

"When-"

She shrugged. "Next couple of days?"

"Phoebe, could I take you for dinner? Thursday evening?" Mike clamped his mouth shut. Where had that come from? Relieved, he realised she was more amused than outraged; her eyes glinting as she suppressed a smile.

"You don't need to do that." She tilted her head to assess him. "I'm happy if I can help."

"But I'd like to."

She chewed her bottom lip, thinking the idea over. "I'm not sure…"

Mike's stomach dropped. She obviously didn't feel the connection as strongly as he did.

"I'd like to," she said slowly then paused. "It's just a bit tricky with my daughter. I've already asked too much from my babysitter recently."

"What about lunch; it doesn't have to be dinner? I could meet you somewhere in town?"

She mulled it over. "That could be good. Yes, ok."

Unphased by the change of plan, he picked up his pint and finished it off.

"I'm sorry to cut and run," Phoebe said, "but I really need to go, it'll take me a good ten minutes to walk back."

"Can I give you a lift, I'm going that way?"

Five minutes later the Range Rover pulled up in front of the Council building and Mike cut the engine.

"Thanks Mike, I could've walked, but this was nice."

"No problem. It gave me an extra ten minutes in your company, and it's on my way."

Her eyes searched his face. "I'd better-" reluctantly she pointed to the Council building.

He wanted to kiss her cheek, drawn in by her floral scent, but he stopped himself; he didn't want to appear too forward.

"So, Thursday just after twelve?" She grabbed her bag from the footwell. "I'll look forward to it."

"Me too," he whispered. They fell silent, looking at each other. Only a couple of feet separated them, and he hardly dared to breathe. Swiftly, she leaned over and dropped a kiss on his cheek. Before he could react, she'd popped the door and climbed out. It happened so quickly he might have thought he'd dreamt it, but when he glanced in the mirror, the lipstick mark on his face proved it had been real.

Phoebe wafted into the office; a grin plastered across her face.

"Someone looks happy," Penny drawled, as she stood to put her jacket on.

"I just met shoe man."

Penny paused and narrowed her eyes. "This is becoming a habit—first last week, then at the weekend."

"A friend of Zina's wanted advice about the right of way, near Gundry's Tower. And low and behold it was him."

Penny grabbed her handbag from the floor and threw the strap over her shoulder. "So?" She hitched her thumb under it.

"There wasn't a lot to tell; so, we're going to meet for lunch on Thursday."

That got Penny's attention and she raised her eyebrows. "I'll bring a packed lunch in, so you can stay out longer -"

Phoebe chuckled, "there's no need for that, an hour will be fine."

Penny studied her co-worker. "Well, the offer's there if you want it. Now, sit yourself down and get on with your work," she laughed. "And take that silly grin off your face," she smiled, waving over her shoulder as she disappeared out for lunch.

Chapter Ten

*E*DDIE'S HAND appeared through the bungalow's attic hatch. She grunted as she eased herself in.

"Careful," warned Tolly, pointing to the floor. "Stick to the boarded areas and you'll be fine. Watch your head."

Eddie levered up to standing and looked round. "It's bigger than I imagined. More messy too," she tutted. "I thought it would be shipshape and *Bristol* fashion."

"Ha, ha, very funny!" He put a hand out and helped her across the boarded platform. "Just because I'm called Bristol, doesn't mean I have to live up to it."

"I would have thought Thea would have insisted on it being tidier."

He glanced across; Eddie didn't talk about his ex-wife very often.

"I assumed she was more fastidious than this; she's always so smart and tidy whenever we see her."

"Yes, well, she might look nice on the outside," he replied, "but we both know she's not as nice as you on the inside." He squeezed Eddie's hand; he knew she felt inadequate in comparison to his ex-wife, but she really had no need to; they were exact opposites and right now he couldn't be happier with his choice. Tolly manoeuvred backwards, keen to stop thinking about his ex-wife. He stooped to avoid hitting his head on a joist and Eddie followed him deeper into the attic. At five foot three, she didn't need to watch where she was going.

"So, what's the plan?" Hands on hips, she surveyed the various boxes and containers scattered around the flooring.

"I thought I'd start to sort it out, you know, in case we finally agree on our living arrangements." He looked at her pointedly. It was a bone of contention, and he was losing hope that they'd ever choose one place to live together. But as they continued to explore their options, he liked the idea of some spring cleaning and the attic was the place to start. He handed Eddie a roll of black bin liners. "I'm expecting a lot of it to go in those, so you hold on to them. If there are any items to keep or be passed on to the family, I'll stack them near the hatch." He clamped his lips together, his face falling. Eddie's hand touched his back and rubbed in a soothing motion.

"You okay to begin this today? It's quite soon after doing the whole of Morris's apartment."

He nodded; a smile flicked briefly across his lips. "I'm fine. I've got the urge to get sorted and find a place for everything."

"—and everything in its place?" Eddie held his gaze, repeating his catch phrase back to him.

"Exactly." He put his arm around her waist and pulled her towards him, kissing her firmly on the lips. "Thank you. Let's give it a go and see how we get on. And don't forget to stick to the boards," he pointed. "If I need to put it on the market buyers won't be keen if there's a ruddy great hole in the ceiling." He earned himself a nudge in the ribs. "Hey! No tomfoolery while we're up here." For a moment they held each other's gaze. "We need to get cracking." He looked at the paraphernalia—years of memories, an indication of a full life—then sighed. "Right! No time like the present."

The first grouping of boxes was straightforward:

Christmas decorations—to keep and sort at a later date ('probably Christmas', Eddie quipped).

A bag full of James' dusty soft toys—to pass to James.

A battered cardboard box of old kitchen equipment—charity shop.

A Fyffes banana box piled to the brim with old Good Housekeeping magazines.

He frowned. Thea must have stored them up here. Why? He wasn't sure. His first wife had never been a keen cook; they could go straight in the recycling bin.

As he sorted, Eddie labelled items and either put them to the side or carried them down the ladder. Her huffs and puffs rose through the hatch as she manoeuvred bags below. They were storing items in the spare room for now and she'd been up and down the ladder several times already. Her head popped up, and she paused, catching her breath.

"This is more tiring than going on a hike." She used her arms to pull herself through, giving a weak cough. "Ugh, it's really dusty up here. I can taste it." She swallowed a couple of times and cleared her throat. Tolly paused in looking through a box, wishing she'd stop interrupting him.

"I could do with a coffee. Do you want one?"

"I'll make it," she offered. "Although you could have said that when I was downstairs… save me climbing the ladder *again*." She harrumphed and disappeared back through the hatch and Tolly straightened, taking a moment to enjoy the quiet. He listened to her movements below, as she bustled around the kitchen opening cupboards. Maybe he should have done this on his own. He scanned the remaining boxes and spotted a scruffy, tall one. It was well-battered and hidden behind a joist. Intrigued, he sat down and slowly stretched out his legs. Inside the box several canvases leaned against each other. He picked them out, one at a time, and propped them against the side. There was a mix of different styles; someone experimenting maybe? There were sketches and pencil drawings; a couple of landscapes in oils, and several were not even finished. He would have thought they were by different people if it wasn't for the same signature in the bottom right-hand corner of each. Diana Tucker. Definitely her early work, as she didn't use her married name now. She preferred to keep her family life private. Tolly couldn't recall ever seeing the box before. He'd have to give them back.

"Hey, slacking off as soon as my back is turned?" Eddie's head appeared. "Could you take the tray, please?"

Tolly grunted as his stiff joints straightened and he took the tray from Eddie, placing it near the paintings.

"What were you looking at?"

He pointed to the pictures.

"Diana's?" Eddie offered him a chocolate biscuit and as they chewed in silence, they looked over the artwork.

"She's good, isn't she?" Eddie murmured in appreciation, between mouthfuls. "And so different, not at all like the huge, contemporary paintings she creates now."

"Although," Tolly pointed towards a couple of oils, "she seems to favour landscapes and nature, rather than people." He leaned an unfinished sketch against the others. It was obviously of James—his hair was longer, with flecks of gold oil, and curled above his collar—but she'd captured his roman nose and the crease between his eyebrows perfectly. Tolly placed a beautiful landscape in front. The majority of which was green; coastal grass and heathland dotted with the most exquisite tiny pink flowers.

"Is that sea, or sky?" Eddie pointed to a sliver of blue at the top of the canvas, turning her head from left to right.

"The sea? Look-" Tolly squinted "-I think that dot might be a boat."

"Um," Eddie tapped her chin. "It looks familiar." She pointed to the far-left hand side where a line of white indicated the stones of a building. "Isn't that the beginnings of Gundry's Tower?"

"I think you're right. I wonder why she didn't focus more on the building?" Tolly looked back at the painting. "James proposed to her by the hedge there, don't you remember, they mentioned it at the weekend?"

Eddie nodded, licking crumbs off her fingers. "It does seem to be one of those places that holds memories, good and bad, for a lot of people."

"Perhaps she was practising how to do landscape. You can almost feel the wind moving through that grass, can't you? It's very realistic."

Eddie tipped her head to one side, as she reached out for another biscuit. "She's a talented girl." The words were whispered, and Tolly had to agree; it was a beautiful painting.

"I'll have to give them back to her. In fact, she's popping round later to borrow my electric drill." He leant in conspiratorially. "They're probably worth a bob or two."

Eddie tutted. "Will you stop worrying about money?"

"I was only joking." He pulled back, as if scolded, and bit into his biscuit.

"I know you were," she softened. "Anyway, *I'll* look after you." She patted his knee and whilst he knew she'd meant it kindly; he bristled. He didn't need to be looked after. Or did he? A lot had changed since he'd shared this house with Thea. He used to be in control then; he'd earnt the money and given Thea a housekeeping budget. He hadn't questioned it; a lot of households operated that way. Now, though, he wondered if Thea would have liked to have worked; he'd never asked her. Maybe, without the pressure of having to provide, he'd have been a bit more laid back… maybe she'd not have ended up resenting him like she did? Water under the bridge now, of course, but it was dawning on him that life with Eddie was going to be, what did they call it now, 'a learning experience.'

"You look very serious. What are you thinking about?" She was also extremely perceptive.

"I was just thinking how different it's going to be for us. I've always held the purse strings and made financial decisions. Maybe I was too old fashioned for Thea; maybe she resented having no say in that. You and Rex, James and Diana, Amir and Heather… when they were together," he added, "all worked and contributed. And you are much more knowledgeable than me about running a house."

She tipped her head from side to side, narrowing her eyes at him. "Are you having second thoughts about us?"

He sat up straight. "No. It's just a lot of change, that's all."

"We'll be fine," she reassured. "As long as you don't start trying to boss me about."

"As if!"

She laughed. "Equal partners. We'll do everything together." She held out her hand and Tolly took it, shaking it slowly up and down.

"Equal partners," he nodded. He carefully replaced the canvases in the box. "I bet Diana will be thrilled to see these again." He shuffled the box over towards the hatch then came back and pulled Eddie to standing.

"See, this trip down memory lane isn't all bad, is it?" She kissed his cheek then gently patted his arm.

"So far, so good. Although we haven't got to the photos yet," he raised his bushy eyebrows. "That could take us ages."

"Oh, my goodness, look at you two." Diana sidestepped as she came in the back door. "No offence but I'll not come any closer, you're filthy." She blew a kiss to each of them but maintained her distance. "Before you say it," she gestured to her own clothing, "I know, I know… I'm filthy too."

"You've been busy by the look of it." Tolly nodded at her paint-splattered sweatshirt and leggings. Her normally unruly hair was pulled back into a tight bun and a bandana prevented any loose hairs from irritating her face. The bun and the bandana were also splashed with different coloured paints. Tolly waved her further into the kitchen and shut the door. "Cup of tea or coffee?"

"Oh." Diana seemed surprised by the offer. "Yes please. Tea would be lovely… if you're having one too?"

Tolly glanced at Eddie who nodded. "Need something to wash the dust down. He's not been up there for years. It's a disgrace." She shook her head in mock disgust.

"So how is it going?" Diana sat on a kitchen chair and was joined at the table by Eddie.

"Slowly. It's not so much the amount of stuff, but he has to check it, then decide. It all takes time. But you're getting there, aren't you, love?"

Tolly nodded then busied himself with the teapot. Diana caught Eddie's eye.

"Is he alright?" she mouthed, putting a thumb in the air, then turning it downwards. Eddie shrugged and waved her palm from side to side.

"So, so", she whispered.

"Here you go." Tolly placed two mugs on the table. "What are you two whispering about?"

"Nothing," Eddie lied. "Just laughing at each other's appearance."

Diana nodded, a picture of innocence, as he pulled a chair next to them and slumped onto it. He ran a hand through his hair, frowning as he found a cobweb. "I'm beginning to sympathise with Indiana Jones in the Temple of Doom." He stood and brushed it off into the bin. "Not seen any scarab beetles but plenty of spiders, cobwebs and dust." He washed his hands and dried them on an 'English Garden Birds' tea towel. "Poor Eddie has been up and down that ladder like..." he re-took his seat and glanced up to the ceiling. "I'm too tired to even think of an analogy."

"Well, you're doing a good job," Diana laughed. "Dare I ask whether there will be anything wending its way to James? I can take stuff now if you want it out the way."

"There is something actually." Tolly made to stand again, but Eddie put a hand on his arm.

"I'll get it. You have your tea." She went out to the hallway. Tolly had placed the box of paintings by the front door and whilst it was bulky, it didn't weigh a lot. He chuckled wearily as she returned, bottom first, dragging the box behind her.

"I believe these might be yours," she said to Diana. She gave one last tug on the cardboard to slide the box across the lino as Diana gasped. She squatted down beside the box and touched it gingerly. "Oh, my goodness. I wondered what had happened to these."

"We must have stored them here when you moved." Tolly was touched by her obvious delight at seeing the paintings again.

"Wow, thank you." She started to flick through them, making a noise at each painting to indicate whether she thought it was good or not. Lost in her memories, she carefully moved each canvas. "Now, this one," she held up the painting of the flowers that Tolly had admired so much. Her eyes took in the detail. "This one is special." She turned it round to show them. "It was for the summer exhibition at the Royal Academy. Once this one had been on display, I started to get more critical attention."

"It is beautiful," Eddie agreed. "That was our favourite. The grass is so realistic."

"I'll have to include that in the exhibition," Diana whispered, tracing a finger over the tiny dots of flowers. Her eyes didn't leave the painting. "Thank you," she repeated before carefully replacing it in the box. She flicked past another few canvases and paused at the portrait of James. "Um." She lifted it out. "Not all of them will be worth saving."

"You can't throw it away," Eddie whispered. "Won't he be offended?"

Diana shrugged. "Maybe he could put it in his study," she wondered aloud.

"Perhaps you could finish it?" Tolly suggested and raised his eyebrows. "Just an idea; when you get time."

Diana glanced at him and nodded slowly, a thought taking root. "That's not a bad idea at all, although time is an issue. Maybe I could finish it for his birthday."

"Talking of James, there is also a bag of toys for him." Tolly looked around the kitchen; he'd put them somewhere safe. Now where were they? As if Eddie could read his mind, she added, "they're in the spare room."

Diana sat back on her chair. "Toys? What sort of toys?"

"Cuddly toys, teddies and the like."

"James had teddies?" A look of disbelief flitted across her face. "I thought he was born cuddling golf clubs."

Tolly shook his head. "There was a time when his bed was covered in soft toys. He wouldn't sleep without Fred or Frog… his favourite teddy and a hideous green frog beanbag." He chuckled at the memory then fell silent, as he realised the two women were watching him. "Yes, well, they're around somewhere if he wants them."

Diana finished her tea and pushed her mug into the centre of the table. "I'm sure he'd love to see them again—and if he doesn't, he can give them to the charity shop." She stood. "Thanks for the tea. I'd better dash."

Tolly pointed down the hallway. "You really want to take them?" He pictured the toys, care-worn and bedraggled; he knew how they felt! They were also very dusty, and he wondered whether they'd be allowed in the house once Diana saw the state of them. But she nodded, a twinkle in her eye.

"Yes, please. I'll put Fred and Frog in our bedroom, see if he notices."

Tolly went to the spare room to collect the bin bag; the two favourites were on the top and he felt a pang of emotion at seeing them. They needed some T.L.C. A good tidy up and they could have years ahead of them—again, rather like himself! He chuckled, suddenly feeling brighter. It was time to close this chapter of his life, put the bungalow on the market and then the next part of his story, with Eddie, could begin. He took a deep breath as a bubble of excitement rose within him and, picking up the bag, he returned to the kitchen.

Chapter Eleven

On Thursday morning, as Phoebe walked across the Council car park, she noticed the lights on in the single-story extension that housed the Archives department. It was a secure, fireproof storage unit where old files and paperwork were held before they were destroyed after the requisite number of years. On a whim, she pushed open the door and an electronic beep announced her arrival. After just a few seconds a young man appeared, a smile breaking out on his face when he saw her.

"Alright Phoebs, you're in early; I've only just got here myself."

"Hi Nicky. I was on my way in and saw the lights."

"How are you?" Standing across the counter, he seemed genuinely pleased to see her.

"Good thanks." She decided not to mention her attempt at promotion. "How about you? All settled in here?" Nicky had been with the Archives department for a few months. Prior to that he'd been an apprentice and had worked his way around a few departments, hers included. He was friendly and extremely switched on. He'd done well to secure this permanent role before the end of his training, and Phoebe had no doubt he'd go far. She'd even coached him for several interviews—the irony of which wasn't lost on her now, as she replayed her own recent woeful interview.

"Yeah, I'm really enjoying it," he grinned, "and I've just got a flat with Maddie-"

"Wow, must be serious."

He blushed and nodded; his eyes gleaming at the mention of his girlfriend.

"How is she getting on with work?"

"Oh man, she loves it. She's at college two days a week now, and in the salon the rest." He struck a pose and touched his hair, waiting for Phoebe to comment. "She's been keeping my mop in trim so she must be alright, I don't let just anyone loose on it," he laughed. His sun-bleached hair was immaculate, the top slightly longer and stuck up an inch, thanks to a generous helping of gel. "She's only got another six months and she'll be qualified."

"I'm really happy for you, both of you." How were some people so organized, with a clear life plan by their early twenties?

"So, what can I do for you or is this a social call?"

"No, 'fraid not. I wanted to find out about the work happening at Gundry's Tower. Thomas—Johnson," she added seeing Nicky's frown, "seems to think that the planning permission is approved, the paperwork now archived." She leant onto the counter. "It's not really work; I'm being nosy. I was there at the weekend and wondered what was going on."

"Let's have a look." Nicky woke the computer and started to tap the keyboard. He shook his head, lips in a firm line. "Nothing coming up for Gundry's—any other name it might be under?"

She gazed out the window. "This is very weird."

He tapped the keys again. "Nothing for Tower Gundry's either."

"He must have it wrong then," she mused, taking a deep breath. "The paperwork must be in the office somewhere. Thanks for looking anyway. I'll let you get back to your work. Nice to catch up with you Nicky."

"Yeah, you too. Don't be a stranger now," he added with an American accent, giving her a quick wave before she left.

Walking along the corridor Phoebe reasoned that if the paperwork wasn't in the filing store, and it wasn't in Archives either, then it must still be with Thomas's admin team. Maybe his secretary hadn't got as far as sending it over to Nicky yet. That was the only possibility she could think of. She paused at the end of the corridor. If she turned right, she'd enter her own open plan office; to the left was the shared space for the admin team, with the offices for Thomas and Roddy Chandler, the Head of Planning, to the side. What the hell? She turned left and entered the admin office, grinning as one of the secretary's looked up.

"Hi Phoebe, how are you?"

They exchanged a few pleasantries before Phoebe turned the conversation to Gundry's.

"Thomas thought the documents were in Archives, but Nicky has no receipt of them." She watched the woman frown, confusion clear on her face.

"Why did Thomas say that?" She flicked through some files on her desk. "There was an Appeal, it came in last week, he knows that." She tutted and looked back to Phoebe. "The file must still be with him," she thumbed over her shoulder, towards his office. "He's in there with Roddy at the moment, but when he's free I'll find out what's going on." She tapped her forehead, remembering. "I'm only in for half a day today, so if I don't come back to you by lunch time, I'll let you know tomorrow."

"Perfect." At last, some progress. "Thank you."

Phoebe waited inside the steamy café; she was halfway down one side of the menu, studying the list of food for the second time, when Mike appeared through the door followed by a blast of fresh air.

"Sorry I'm late." He bent to kiss her cheek, and she caught a whiff of spicy citrus aftershave. She inhaled, the couple of times she'd seen him he'd always smelt nice. She spied on him as he removed his waxed jacket and hung it over the chair. Jeans and a blue shirt today; casual but very well put together. She liked clothes and what they symbolised about the person; she wondered what he thought of her red three-quarter length trousers and navy-blue polka dot blouse.

"You look lovely," he said quietly, as if reading her thoughts. "Spotty." He laughed, his hand gesturing to her top, "the polka dots!" His laughter was light, carefree, and she grinned.

"I can't deny, I *love* a polka dot pattern."

"They suit you." His eyes lingered on hers and she found herself being drawn to him; there was something magnetic about his blue eyes. She could happily sit here and stare into them for her whole lunch break.

"Uh-huh," a young lad shuffled next to the table, clearing his throat to get their attention. Phoebe snapped back to the present.

"Have you decided what you'd like?" The waiter refused to make eye contact with either of them, fascinated by his biro which hovered over a clean page of his notepad. He waited for their order, then ambled off to pass their choices to the kitchen. Phoebe felt for him and his awkwardness, then looked up to find Mike watching.

"So," Mike took a deep breath, "how's your week been?"

"Alright so far-"

"Better than last week?"

"-*definitely* better than last week." She smiled, touched that he was interested. "Although I haven't been able to find out much about Gundry's Tower yet, I'm hoping to know more tomorrow." She'd need to get an update.

Mike shrugged. "I'm not just seeing you to find out about Gundry's-"

"You're not?" she toyed, then felt awful when she noticed a frown flick across his forehead.

"I thought we...," he waved his hands between them, but they were interrupted by the arrival of their drinks; Phoebe sipped her cordial while they waited for the waiter to leave.

"I like you, Phoebe," he said quietly "and besides, I've been making a few enquiries of my own so between us we'll find out what's going on."

The way he said 'us' gave her a warm fuzzy feeling. She realised she'd not enjoyed much adult company recently, with the exception of Agnes next door, and she relaxed as he told her about his work, asking her questions about hers. They enjoyed a club sandwich, and shared some chips before, glancing at her watch, she pulled a face.

"I really should get going. I'm sorry," she added. "I always seem to be running off, don't I?"

"I have that effect on women."

"I can't believe that for one moment," she laughed. "I imagine you're hounded." A pang of jealousy stabbed at her as she imagined a group of women chasing after him. For a moment he paused; he looked conflicted as if about to say something and Phoebe waited. Then he sniffed, a smile lit his face and he shook his head.

"You're so wrong," he chuckled, "and even if that were true, I've not been interested in anything like that-"

"Oh?"

"-until now."

"Oh," she repeated, this time a whisper. "Who would that lucky lady be?"

He raised his eyebrows, then cleared his throat. "The Wanderers are meeting on Saturday to walk to Gundry's again. I'm going to take a drone and fly it over the site to see what's happening. Would you and your daughter like to come with us?"

"Oh, I don't know."

She wasn't sure about introducing Celeste to him yet but, sensing her reticence, he added, "there will be a few of us going; I'm not sure if Sadiq is coming but Rita has said yes."

Phoebe raised her eyebrows; that put a different slant on it. She mulled it over; it could be fun. She'd really enjoyed getting outdoors again with the Brownies and if Rita was going, it'd be a group outing rather than a date. "Let me check a few things first, then I'll give you a bell. Shall I take your number?"

They exchanged details and as Mike offered to pay for lunch, Phoebe headed back to work with a new spring in her step.

Phoebe stared at the plastic clock on the kitchen wall as she waited for the kettle to boil at work. Only an hour to go and she could head home. She'd offered to do the tea run; she needed a caffeine injection to get through the dragging afternoon. She was keen to leave on time today as she was planning to call in and see Rita. She wanted to check on the details about Saturday, to make sure it would be suitable for Celeste. She put the two full mugs on a circular tray and was just about to manoeuvre out the door when it opened, and Thomas walked in.

"Ah good. Penny said you were here."

Phoebe straightened, holding the tray. She waited for him to continue.

"I understand you've been asking about Gundry's Tower *again*." The way he emphasized 'again' made her feel like a troublesome child.

"That's right," she said more confidently than she felt.

He took a deep breath and shook his head. "I said it was all sorted; I can't understand why you are so interested."

She felt her cheeks heating up and shrugged. "I just wanted to find out what was happening there."

"I've *told* you; Queen's Hill care home is having additional accommodation built and it was all agreed ages ago."

"I'd heard there had been an appeal."

His eyes flicked up. He stared at her, his pupils dilating as he clenched his jaw. She took a step back towards the kitchen counter.

"No, it's all been sorted and archived."

"But it's *not* in Archives," she said, before she could stop herself. She paused, then added quietly, "I checked."

"You checked?" He took a step towards her, breathing loudly through his nose. He appeared to be thinking then sneered. "Well, if the file's not there it must be in transit. The appeal was denied, and the work is going ahead." He turned towards the door then paused and looked back. "You know, at this time when we need to make savings within the Council, everyone's keeping their heads down in case of redundancies." He raised his eyebrows at her. "Everyone, that is, except you." He tutted, shaking his head. "Don't take this the wrong way, but you'd do better to get on with your work, rather than poking your nose into other people's business."

Her stomach dropped. Was he threatening her? Surely, he wouldn't be that obvious.

"I just thought it would be a matter of public record," she tried to justify her actions. "I wasn't poking my nose in," she whispered. She was conscientious and hardworking; she knew her place and she certainly wasn't out to make trouble.

"I'm sure it's all been recorded, so don't worry yourself about it."

Before she could think of anything to say the door opened and Penny's bobbed hair-do appeared round the door.

"There you are," she grinned at them, oblivious to the charged atmosphere. "I wondered where you'd gone."

Thomas ignored her and continued to look at Phoebe. "Do we understand each other?"

Unable to speak Phoebe stared at him, her head spinning with his words and threats. With a curt nod towards Penny, Thomas marched out of the kitchen.

"What did he want?" She whispered as soon as the door shut.

"Oh," Phoebe struggled to think of something, "just checking about the minutes from a recent meeting," she gabbled, flashing a smile at Penny. "Sorry, come on, let's get these teas back, before they go cold."

Chapter Twelve

Striding at pace along the High Street, Phoebe replayed the conversation over and over in her head. Whatever way she repeated the words, it still sounded like she was in trouble. Her stomach lurched each time she considered how he might use it against her, particularly if she had to fight to keep her job during the current round of cuts. She tried to pull her mind back to the beautiful evening; to the bird song ringing out from every hedge she passed on her short walk back home. She was concentrating so hard, replaying the conversation again for the hundredth time, that she almost forgot to turn into Rita's street.

Phoebe had been in Rita's terraced cottage twice before and each time it was like stepping into a make-believe world. The tiny door gave way to a cluttered, cosy front room. Phoebe ducked her head to avoid low beams and kept a hand on her shoulder bag to prevent it from swinging round and knocking ornaments from side tables. Phoebe was shorter and thinner than Rita, and she was fascinated at how the older woman could bustle about with such ease amongst the furniture and objects; she must be so familiar with the layout that she didn't pay any attention as she beckoned Phoebe through the back and into the kitchen. Rita led the way, her outdoor trousers rustling as she moved to the next room. This place was the complete opposite to the first. It had been extended upwards and outwards to create a light, glass atrium. The kitchen cupboards were a smooth glossy grey, and while the counters housed the essentials, such as kettle, toaster and a coffee machine, there was none of the clutter from the front room. The contrast was stark.

Beyond the glass lay a small circular patio which gave way to a rising garden. There were three terraces full of woodland plants and ferns, but no grass to be seen. Each time Phoebe came here it was like stepping into an enchanted woodland; she half expected to spy fairies sitting on toadstools when she looked out.

"Your garden is amazing." She walked up to the glass doors and peered through.

"Thanks." Rita filled the kettle and invited Phoebe to sit at the wooden table next to the window. "I spend a lot of time out there, and then in here staring out, when it gets colder."

"Every bit of space is crammed; it must take ages to weed."

"Ah well," Rita switched the kettle on and lifted two mugs from a cupboard. "That's the beauty of it. I've done the planting so that they all flower at different times, following on from each other. Because it's so crammed together the weeds don't get a chance to break through."

"Very clever." Phoebe continued to stare outside. "Of course, if *you* can't get your planting right, Professor, then goodness help the rest of us," she joked and turned to see Rita grabbing a teapot. She joined her at the table, and they sat in companionable silence while Rita mashed the tea; they both preferred it strong.

"So, to what do I owe this pleasure? I hear you've seen Mike a couple of times this week." Rita raised her eyebrows, clearly enjoying the fact that she'd caught Phoebe off guard.

"Word travels fast in this town, doesn't it?" Phoebe said, laughing when Rita wiggled her eyebrows.

"Particularly among the Wanderers."

"Of course."

"No, we don't really gossip; the only reason he mentioned it was because he said you might join us on Saturday, with Celeste?"

"That's partly why I've called round. Is it going to be suitable for Celeste, and me for that matter?"

Rita poured the tea and pushed one of the mugs across the table.

"Sure, it'll be suitable," Rita nodded. "We'll meet at the Visitors centre. In fact, you and Celeste could come here and get a lift with me. We'll walk back up to Gundry's from the other side to last time. We're normally out from ten until three ish, it should be good, and the weather looks nice."

"Will the other Wanderers mind if Celeste and I just come along?"

Rita looked affronted at the idea. "Why would they mind? The more the merrier." She slurped at her tea, pulling away sharply, "ouch that's hot." She put the mug on the table and looked at Phoebe. "It'll be nice to have…" she paused, considering her choice of words, "younger members of the group. It's good to have a spread of ages and you enjoyed last weekend, didn't you?"

Phoebe nodded. "I really did, more than I'd imagined."

"There'll also be the added bonus of Mike being there." She was back to wiggling her eyebrows then lowered her voice. "He seems very keen for us to make a good impression."

"Does he?" Phoebe felt a fluttering in her stomach, it seemed to occur whenever anyone mentioned Mike's name, which was quite frequently at the moment. Rita nodded. "He does. He's organised us into bringing items for a picnic and an array of drinks. He's also planned a geocache for Celeste-"

Phoebe frowned.

"-Like a treasure hunt," Rita explained. "People hide small trinkets all over the place and mark them with directions on an App. You must hunt for each one, using the coordinates and clues given, and if you find the box you can take one thing from it, replacing it with one of your own treasures. It's good fun; we should try it with the Brownies—I don't know why I haven't thought of that before," she paused. "See," she picked up her mug again, "I'm already getting a different perspective because of new members."

"I bet Celeste would love that."

"You're going to come then?"

Phoebe nodded. "I think we might, thanks."

"You're welcome."

They both blew on their tea and sipped at the strong brown liquid, gazing out to the fairy glen beyond.

"I also wanted to see if you'd been able to find anything out about Gundry's, from your contacts."

Rita shook her head. "I've mentioned it to a few people, but it was as much a surprise to them as it was to us. You?"

Phoebe shook her head. "Afraid not. But I had a really strange run in with Thomas Johnson though."

"Oh?"

Phoebe explained all about the trip to Archives and the subsequent conversation with Thomas in the kitchen. "I know I'm not the savviest when it comes to business politics, but it felt like he was warning me off."

"What did he say?"

"He mentioned potential cost savings and he said about job cuts too, telling me to get on with my work rather than poking my nose in-"

"Did he say, 'poking your nose in'?"

Phoebe nodded. "I've gone over and over it in my head since and he definitely did."

"What did you say?"

"Not a lot, I was too taken aback. If Penny hadn't interrupted I don't know what would have happened."

Rita sat back against her chair and cradled her mug. Her face was neutral. "He likes to antagonise people doesn't he, Mr. Johnson?"

"Why, what else has he done?"

"He's been contracting work elsewhere."

"What, not to you?"

Rita shook her head. "I haven't done any surveys for the Council for a good few months now."

"Really?" This was news to Phoebe. "But I thought you held the contract with them?"

"I do. It makes me wonder where they are going."

"Well, that should be easy enough to find out, shouldn't it?"

Rita frowned. "How do you mean?"

"It should be a matter of public record."

"What, like the planning permission and the appeal information, which we can't find out anything about?" Rita shrugged, her eyes on Phoebe, and she saw her point. There was something underhand about Gundry's Tower, and if Rita hadn't been doing any surveys, then who had; in fact, had *anyone*? And what about the other developments that were happening around the County?

The questions milled around Phoebe's head on the short walk back home. She tried to block them out, repeating Thomas's warning to concentrate on her own work and not go 'poking her nose in' about other things. Perhaps she was getting involved in areas that shouldn't concern her. Normally, she knew her limitations and she didn't overstep boundaries. Opening her gate, she looked up at the front of her house. Her home. She needed her job, for the sake of her mortgage and this place, and therefore, perhaps, she should heed his advice.

The questions continued to spin round her head as she climbed into bed later that evening; she'd decided to go early to read her book and to still her thoughts. She needed something else to think about but, so far, it wasn't working. Her phone beeped on the bedside table and picking it up she saw a text from Mike.

Hi there, lovely to see you earlier.
Just wondered if you'd thought any more
about coming on Saturday.
It'll be good fun, I promise.

She smiled, recalling Rita's words earlier about Mike trying to organize everything.

Hi Mike, you too.
Yes, Celeste and I would love to come on Saturday.
I saw Rita this evening and she mentioned
geo-cache?? Sounds fun.

Brilliant. Want me to pick you up?

No need. Rita has offered. We'll get to
the Visitors Centre for 10am.

Okay. See you Saturday.
Look forward to it, and to meeting Celeste properly.
M xx

See you Saturday.
P xx

She clutched the phone to her chest, her heart beating a jig. He was looking forward to meeting Celeste properly. She needed to play this cool and not jump in with both feet. She put the phone on the bedside table and switched off her light, settling down beneath the covers. She stared at the ceiling, her thoughts flitting to Mike; his smile in the café, their easy-going conversation, his concern over getting the picnic right, geo-caching for Celeste. She closed her eyes and smiled. Keep it cool, she reminded herself, although Rita seemed to think he was nice. Rita. That made her think about work, and her mind switched to an image of Thomas Johnson. As she lay in bed mulling over the day, she wondered why, out of all the rights of way in the county, he was so interested in that one. Her eyes opened and she stared into the dark. There was no light visible except for a tiny stripe of moonlight shining below the curtains. Something about this didn't add up and it was making her Spidey-senses tingle—but at this moment in time, she wasn't quite sure why.

Chapter Thirteen

As Phoebe walked up her path on Friday, she spotted Agnes and Celeste sitting on the front step.

"Everything okay?" Her heart quickened, as the two of them stopped their conversation and turned to face her.

"Oh hello, love," Agnes pushed herself up with a groan and turned to help Celeste. Too late, the little girl was already up. She hopped down to meet her mum and wrapped her arms around Phoebe's middle. Feeling the little body crush against hers had the effect of reducing her heartbeat to a more sustainable level, as she realised the two of them were fine.

"We knew you'd be back soon," Agnes brushed her trousers to get rid of any grit she might have picked up from the step. "We thought we'd sit in the sun and wait for you."

The little girl was hanging off her mum, being dragged along the path towards the door.

"Let your mum go, you daftie," Agnes chuckled at the youngster, "She needs to get in the door." Agnes tickled her under the armpits and Celeste gave in, unhooking her arms.

"Thank you!" Phoebe turned her key and pushed the door open allowing Celeste to sneak through. She threw her school bag under the stairs, earning a tut of disapproval from both women, as Phoebe waved Agnes into the house. "Cup of tea?"

"That would be nice. Shall I put the kettle on?" Agnes walked down the hall towards the kitchen at the back.

"Can I have a biscuit?" Celeste trailed along after her and Phoebe smiled a weary smile as she bent over with a groan to unbuckle her shoes. As she stepped out, she wriggled her toes, allowing them to stretch on the cool patterned tiles. She hung her coat from the newel post then thought better of it, lifting it to hang it properly on one of the understairs hooks. She could hardly moan at Celeste for being untidy if she didn't make the effort too. Celeste passed her in the hallway, nibbling on a biscuit.

"I'll hang up my uniform, don't worry," she mumbled through crumbs and Phoebe nodded.

"Good girl. I'll be in the kitchen." She wandered through to see Agnes sitting at the table, the teapot and mugs already out. "That was quick work." She took a seat opposite, sliding along the bench seat to face Agnes.

"Love, I've got something to show you." Grinning, Agnes produced an envelope from a trouser pocket and slid it over the table. "I've been so excited; I could hardly wait to tell you."

Intrigued, Phoebe lifted the letter, noticing the BBC stamp on the top of the thick, expensive envelope. She glanced at Agnes, who nodded for her to open it. She looked as if she might burst with excitement so, doing as she was told, Phoebe pulled out the typed letter and began to read aloud.

> *"Dear Mrs Greystone,*
>
> *As you may be aware, each year the BBC hosts an evening to celebrate the best of the industry, honouring those who have made outstanding contributions to the development of the industry.*
>
> *Due to the revival of 'Drop Your Balls-'"*

Phoebe laughed. She paused and looked at Agnes for an explanation, but Agnes just nodded at the letter, urging her to continue reading.

> *"Due to the revival of 'Drop Your Balls-'"*

she stifled a giggle,

> *"We'd like to invite you and a guest to this annual event to share in the success of this show as we look back on its history and the significant role played by your husband, Albert-"*

Agnes tutted, "he hated being called Albert."
Phoebe continued,

> *"It would be our honour to look after you and your guest for the evening and if you'd like to discuss the details, please don't hesitate to contact my assistant Carrie on telephone number…blah, blah, blah."*

Phoebe dropped the letter on the table and looked over at Agnes. "What's that mean, Agnes?"

Before her neighbour got the opportunity to reply, Celeste skidded into the kitchen and banged against the fridge.

"Celeste darling, shush." Phoebe looked over. "Get some milk and come and sit down. Agnes is telling us a story."

Agnes gathered the letter and once Celeste had slid onto the bench next to her mum, she started to talk.

"Isn't it brilliant?" Her eyes shone as one hand stroked the letter. "Bert would have loved this. He worked so hard on that show and now because of J.J. Stewart, it's back in fashion."

"Agnes, what did Bert have to do with 'Drop your balls'?"

Agnes sighed and smiled at the two people sitting opposite.

"My Bert used to work for the BBC."

Phoebe waved her hand, wanting to get to the point.

"He worked on many shows," Agnes continued, "some of them did well, some not so. They ranged from regional news shows at the beginning to some bigger shows later—'Come Dancing' was one. That's where I met Bruno." She drifted off as memories overtook her. "Anyway," she came back to the present, "Bert came up with the idea for 'Drop Your Balls'-"

Phoebe's mouth fell open. The game show was one of the biggest things on TV, hosted by J.J. Stewart who was a firm favourite with the general public. Once a member of a boy band, J.J. was now much in favour with the BBC. 'Drop Your Balls' had been his first major success since leaving The Tin Boys and the ratings for the show were huge. It was now being pushed out at a rate of a series each year.

"I never knew that."

"He wasn't proud of it-" Agnes lowered her voice.

"Why?" Phoebe was incredulous. "It's a great show."

"It bombed back in the 80s. The first series was met with a lukewarm reception, but the BBC commissioned a second with Davie Green. It had such bad viewing figures that it was pulled halfway through. It was a bad time," she shook her head. "Bert was beside himself and from there he moved into production and tried to forget the whole sorry episode."

"He was obviously ahead of his time," soothed Phoebe, putting her hand over the older lady's and squeezing it. "If only he knew how we'd all love it now."

Agnes smiled sadly and in return, patted Phoebe's hand. "Yep." She took a sharp intake of breath. "And now, look! An invitation to a glitzy night. I don't know what to do."

"You should go," Phoebe urged. "He developed it and you should be there to make sure he gets the respect he deserves."

"I don't know love."

Phoebe looked appalled. "Don't know! A super swanky night and you're thinking about turning it down. Are you mad?"

"Will you come with me?"

"Can I come?" Celeste paused mid biscuit, looking hopefully between the two women.

"I think it's for adults only darling," Phoebe pulled an apologetic face at her daughter, "but we'll tell you all about it after. Perhaps you could have a sleepover at Toby's?" Celeste's eyes lit up at the mention of her best friend.

"You'll come?" Agnes looked at Phoebe.

"Of course I'll come! We'll have to get new dresses and get our hair done."

"And your nails," Celeste piped up, getting excited on their behalf.

"Are you sure?" Agnes looked at Phoebe.

"A night hobnobbing with the stars? Just you try to keep me away," she laughed.

Chapter fourteen

As Mike pulled into the Visitors centre car park on Saturday morning, his attention was drawn to a group congregated near the paying machine. They turned as the car approached and he waved in their direction; a broad smile breaking out across his face. The sun was shining, there was a good attendance by the group, and he had several gadgets with him to keep everyone entertained. He frowned; he couldn't see Phoebe among them, but Rita was there talking to Eddie. He locked his car and walked over, eager to find out if there'd been a change of plan.

"Mike!"

He turned towards the Visitors centre and his heart lifted as he spotted Phoebe. She was waving with one hand and holding Celeste's with the other. They were here! Now it really was a perfect day.

"I thought you weren't coming for a moment," he pointed back to the main group. Phoebe smiled, gently shaking Celeste's hand.

"This one needed to pop inside." She motioned towards the toilets and rolled her eyes. "Likes to check everything out, don't you Celeste?"

"Very sensible," he agreed, and the little girl nudged into Phoebe's leg, her big brown eyes looking shyly up at Mike.

"Celeste, this is Mike, my new friend that I was telling you about."

Mike held his hand out and Celeste reluctantly lifted hers, allowing a weak handshake.

"Very pleased to meet you, Celeste," he nodded his head. "I've heard a lot about you from your mum." He leant towards her and whispered, "actually she doesn't stop talking about you; 'Celeste this, Celeste that,'" he mimicked, and the little girl giggled. "Have you met the others?" He directed the question to Celeste, who shook her head.

She mumbled, "We know Brown Owl, don't we mama?" They started to walk towards the group, "and we saw some people near Gundry's last week."

"Oh yes, your Brownie camp. How was it, was it good?"

Celeste nodded slowly, glancing over at her mum who watched their interaction.

"I think you'll like them," Mike was still talking to her, "shall we go and say hello?" Mike quickly made the introductions. "Eddie, Tolly, Heather."

Celeste peered out as he went around the group.

"You know Rita-"

"Yes, she's Brown Owl."

"And you know Sadiq, Rita's friend?" Phoebe nodded, smiling 'hello' to them as Mike continued around the group.

"This is Heather, she is Eddie's little girl."

Heather swiped at his arm and tutted; Mike rubbed where she'd hit, sticking his bottom lip out. "Well, you are," he said indignantly.

"About thirty years ago," Heather laughed, and Mike saw Celeste beam at her mum, as everyone greeted her. He hoped they were making a good impression as, for some reason, it really mattered. So far, so good.

Tolly stepped forward and adjusted his rucksack. "Right, if everyone is ready, shall we head to the coast path and follow the diversion around Gundry's Tower?"

As the group started to move off, Mike tapped his head remembering something.

"Nearly forgot, parking ticket. And I've got something that might be of interest once we get nearer the diversion."

Tolly tutted. "Come along Mike, get organized."

Eddie nudged him, and Mike smiled a grateful thanks. Why was Tolly so impatient to get going? Then he glanced at his watch and realised it was already gone ten o'clock.

"You start, I'll catch you up. I won't be long." He looked at Phoebe. "You happy to go, just follow Rita?"

"They'll be fine with us," Eddie said, and waved for Phoebe to join her. Rita held her hand out for Celeste who, skipping over, took it and hopped away. Phoebe glanced over her shoulder and shrugged, making Mike laugh. He'd been worried about her fitting in with the group; if he wasn't quick, it would be him left out, not the two new arrivals. He jogged over to his car to collect his backpack and the gadget he'd brought for later.

Celeste stopped and rummaged around in her rucksack.

"You okay, Cel? What are you looking for?" Phoebe had been walking at the back of the group with Mike. Their conversation hadn't faltered in the hour they'd been moving but she, along with all the Wanderers, had been keeping an eye on Celeste who skipped on ahead.

"Just looking for my books." She threw her rucksack to the floor and crouched down, her hand inside. She pulled out two books and looked at the covers.

"Crikey, how many have you got?" Mike stopped next to her.

"Four... ah, here it is." She put one on the floor and re-packed the others.

"Seabirds, good choice for round here."

"And I've got Creepy Crawlies, Moths and Butterflies, and Wildflowers too."

"Sounds good." Mike helped her on with her rucksack. Once it was back in place, she turned her attention to the book and took out a pencil from its holder on the spine.

"I see." Mike watched her as she flicked through the pages. "You tick off the ones you've seen."

Celeste nodded.

"Out of interest, what do you get in the book, just a photo and description?"

She nodded again, making a tick against the picture of a seagull. She closed the book and skipped on, pulling her mum behind her. Phoebe glanced over with an apologetic shrug and, smiling, Mike waved her on. Celeste's books had given him an idea and as he watched them in front, he recognized the familiar feeling of when an idea struck. He pondered on it as he followed, at the rear of the group. He'd been contemplating what projects he'd like to work on next. The contract with the military would tick on to something else once the drone was completed, but a bubble of interest rose inside him as he thought of a different direction for his work; something slightly more frivolous and fun. Educational gadgets for kids—could that work? He mulled over the other books Celeste had brought in her rucksack and whilst the babble of conversation ahead of him continued, he was happy to walk on his own, allowing the ideas to wash around his brain. He fished out his phone and recorded a quick voice note to capture his thoughts. As he put his phone away, he chastised himself; work was always at the forefront of his mind. He rolled his shoulders, trying to loosen them, and reminded himself that today was about having fun in the outdoors and *not* work. He found it very difficult to switch off, but he needed to get better at it if he was serious about having a personal life *as well* as a thriving business. The path began to narrow; to the right, a cliff fell away to the water and rocks below. On the left, low scrub had developed into a sizeable hedge and as the path narrowed, a wooden stile marked a pinch point, but allowed them to pass through a gap in the barbed wire. Mike jogged to catch them up.

"Hey, you know Paul Weller?"

"From The Jam? Of course." Heather, waiting in line, turned to look at him.

Tolly groaned. "Here we go. I thought it was too good to be true." Eddie bumped him with her shoulder, pointing at the stile.

"Well, since retiring from music he's now in charge of agreeing where all these go." Mike pointed at the wooden structure, as Eddie paused at the top, frowning.

"Really?"

"Yes," he chuckled, "he's in The Stile Council." He drummed his hands on his thighs and looked at them all expectantly.

Eddie tutted and swung her leg up. "Does Phoebe know about your propensity for telling bad jokes?"

It was Tolly's turn to climb up. He stood on the top step and looked at Mike. "She does now," he interjected, "although—taking them all into consideration—some are better than others." He jumped down on the other side.

"That's praise indeed," Mike mock whispered as they waited for Celeste to climb the steps and Phoebe caught Mike's eye.

"Stile council," she sniggered, "I'll have to tell my dad that, he used to love Paul Weller. Do you have anymore?"

From the other side of the structure, they heard Tolly groan. Mike held her hand as she climbed over, adding, "I do actually. Oh," his face clouded over. "I didn't tell you; I had some news from my doctor the other day."

Phoebe turned, suddenly serious.

"She said I had the worst case of the 'peeker-boo' virus she'd ever seen." Phoebe narrowed her eyes at him.

"I'll be transferred to I.C.U. next week," he said. He repeated *I.C.U* in a sing-song voice then, "peeker-boo?"

"Ohhh." Phoebe groaned, getting the joke. She jumped down and rolled her eyes at Celeste. The little girl giggled at her funny face and held her hand out.

"Indeed," cautioned Tolly, "I'm afraid you do have to take the rough with the smooth" and snickering, they walked on. Mike watched them go; had he blown it? He was determined to keep his mouth shut; he didn't want Phoebe to think he was immature, but then she looked back, her eyes shining in amusement and motioned for him to catch up.

He was trying to think of some more puns to tell them when suddenly his attention snapped back to the group. The Wanderers had stopped; a line of hoarding was now between them and the rest of the path. Garish yellow metal signs announced 'Diversion' and pointed back inland.

"What a shame, it's still here." Sadness flitted across Eddie's face. "It's such a beautiful view from just over there." She jabbed her finger to highlight the point just out of reach. "Why are they closing so much of it off?"

"I might be able to help with that." Having temporarily forgotten about his potential next project, Mike came back to the present and pulled his rucksack round to extract a box. Everyone crowded in to see what looked like some sort of Star Wars toy, and Mike handed it to Celeste. "Would you like a go with this?"

Celeste took it, turning it over cautiously in her hand.

"What is it?" She nudged in closer to Mike.

"It's a small drone… not as good as the military grade one I used last time," he added, looking at Tolly "but it'll be fun for Celeste to try."

"Celeste?" Phoebe looked alarmed. "I don't know about that," her eyebrows knitted together as she caught Mike's eye.

"It's fine," he patted her arm. "It's an old one from the workshop, honestly."

Celeste was watching her mum, waiting for her reaction.

"Honestly," he repeated. "It doesn't matter if it gets battered."

"Are you sure?" She didn't sound convinced, but he nodded at Celeste, causing her to jump for joy.

"Okay then," Mike spoke to Celeste. "Let's give you some instruction on how to fly this thing." He sat down with her and placed the drone on the ground between them.

Eddie beckoned Phoebe over. "Shall we have a coffee while they get it going?" They sat on the grass and Eddie took a flask from her bag. "We may as well have a break." Phoebe took the proffered mug and biscuit. She dunked the bourbon biscuit in the hot liquid and nibbled at the mushy edges, whilst Mike showed Celeste the basics of operating the machine. Celeste was hanging on his every word, as he pointed to the four rotors and explained about the camera hub in the middle. She caught snatches of words like 'connection', 'wireless', and 'images' before he pointed to his phone where she saw an image of his hand as he lifted the drone up. Celeste nodded excitedly and the two of them stood, watched by the others. The motors started to whir, and the drone lifted off unsteadily from the ground. Celeste and Mike high-fived each other then slowly walked along the diverted path, following the drone whilst watching the controller in front of Celeste. Mike walked by her side, calmly instructing her as the drone dipped and soared overhead. All the time, his phone received the images being sent back. The tiny motor hummed in the background and Phoebe found it strangely relaxing after the initial adrenalin spike that had whooshed through her body; she needed to forget how expensive and fragile the equipment was and have more trust in her daughter.

"He's having so much fun." Eddie spoke with a hand in front of her mouth to prevent biscuit crumbs from spraying out. "He's found a partner in crime-"

"At last," Tolly laughed.

"Exactly," agreed Eddie. "I'm afraid we haven't always been that interested in his machines."

"Does he like his tech then?"

Eddie and Tolly exchanged glances and Phoebe wondered what she was missing.

"You know he's an inventor?" Tolly asked and she nodded.

"Yes, George mentioned something… my friend's cousin works for him."

"He invents all sorts, including high-tech gadgets for the military."

"Tolly!" Eddie glared at him.

"Oops."

"Shush. I'm not sure you should be saying anything."

Tolly mimed zipping his mouth. "Perhaps you're right," he whispered, "he works, with all sorts of people," he seemed to be backtracking. "He's quite a clever person, but don't ever tell him I said that" he laughed. "We like to keep this rivalry going; I pretend he's stupid and he keeps trying to impress me. It works well. I'm sure it's good for his development too."

Eddie and Phoebe laughed.

"I tell you one thing he did invent which was absolutely wonderful," Tolly continued then added, "but again, if you say anything I'll deny all knowledge of this conversation."

Now Phoebe mimed zipping her mouth.

"Touché!" Tolly laughed. "He designed a heat pad for medical use. I had a hip operation last year and I couldn't sleep because of the pain. Mike had invented these heat pads… they were about this big," Tolly held his hands out to indicate a DVD-sized box. "When you removed the backing, a chemical reaction heated the pad up. They were fabulous; they relieved the pain for hours, without the need for drugs." He rubbed his hip as he recalled their use. "I swear they speeded up my recovery; honestly they were marvellous." Tolly wandered away closer to Mike and Celeste to see what they were up to. Phoebe turned to watch Mike; he certainly seemed to be a man of many talents.

"He's good with her, isn't he?" Eddie nodded to where Mike was patiently pointing to something on the controller; the two of them had their heads together. "It's not just *her* he's taken a shine to," she whispered, "he hasn't stopped talking about you all week." Phoebe nibbled the corner of her lip. Except for Rita, she'd not known these people for very long, but it gave her a warm glow to think that Mike had been talking about her. He'd certainly been occupying a lot of her thoughts as well. Celeste and Mike wandered backwards towards them, Celeste concentrating intensely on the control panel as she sent the drone further away, out towards the sea.

"Not too far," Phoebe whispered, unable to stop herself, as Mike looked up to the sky. The drone hummed in the distance, now barely visible as a little black dot out over the water.

"What do you think?" Mike hopped up and down next to them, looking at Tolly. Tolly bit his lip to suppress a smile.

"It serves its purpose, Mike."

Eddie tutted next to him. "It's excellent, Mike. He won't ever tell you, but I think he likes it." She nudged Tolly's arm. "Go on, say something nice, it won't hurt you."

"Yes, like I said, serves its purpose."

"It's so quiet," Eddie enthused. "You'd never know it was there. And the images are superb."

"Bring it back a little, Celeste." Mike looked at the control panel and pointed to the map on screen. "Fly it over there. That's where the Tower is. See if you can find a route for us around the edge." Phoebe leaned her head towards the screen. Land came into view, as the drone flew past them and inland towards the Tower.

"What's that?" Phoebe pointed to the images on Mike's phone.

"Looks like cars… and people."

Celeste moved the joystick and the drone dropped to get a better view.

"Carpenter construction; that's the company we saw last week," Mike murmured. Along with the truck, four people appeared on screen as the picture swam into focus. Suddenly the four of them looked up, directly into the camera.

"Oops, pull it higher, Celeste. We don't want to annoy them." Mike took a step closer; on the alert, ready to take back control if he needed to.

"Who are they?" Eddie shuffled closer; the Wanderers now gathered in a tight circle to watch the screen.

"Builders?" Mike suggested and shrugged his shoulders. Phoebe stared at the screen. She moved in even closer.

"Mama, move your head -" Celeste protested, but Phoebe looked up, her face serious.

"Go down again," she pointed.

"We shouldn't antag-" Mike started, but Phoebe held up her hand.

"I know exactly who that is," she pointed to one of the four. Overweight, the man wore a disheveled suit, its jacket straining across his shoulders. "That's my boss, Thomas Johnson," she said quietly. "Why is he here on a Saturday morning?"

"You know him?" Eddie looked surprised then clicked her fingers. "Of course, I forgot you work at the Council."

Phoebe frowned; it *could* be a coincidence. She chewed her lip, lost in thought.

"You alright?" Mike touched her arm.

She nodded.

"You don't look very sure."

"It's just…" she paused, "You know I was asking about the closure of the path-"

They lifted their heads, and Mike nodded; he'd relayed the information to them.

"Thomas… him," Phoebe pointed, "collared me in an office the other day and was asking me all sorts of questions about it. And now he's here."

"Maybe he's here in an official capacity."

"On a Saturday?"

"He looks quite formal," Mike squinted at the screen. "He *is* wearing a suit."

Um, perhaps she was over thinking it.

"He might have come to make sure the diversion is in the right place," Tolly suggested, but Phoebe wasn't convinced. They didn't know Thomas Johnson like she did. While she mulled over his surprise appearance, Celeste directed the joystick and flew the drone back to them. With thoughts still going round her head, Phoebe watched as Celeste landed the gadget on the floor in front of her feet.

"Wow, you've mastered that." Mike picked it up. "Shall we put it away, and have another go later?"

"Sure. It can have a rest, just for now." Celeste began to pack it away. She managed to fit all the parts in the requisite sections, enabling the lid to slide back into place perfectly.

"You should work on my packing line," Mike joked, "good job."

They high fived and Celeste seemed to grow a tiny bit taller under his praise. Phoebe smiled, her heart squeezing at his kindness. She should concentrate on Mike for now and forget about not-to-be trusted Thomas bloody Johnson.

Celeste led the group around the side of the fencing. She followed the regularly spaced diversion signs, as the route took them inland and away from any hope of a coastal view. They wandered along a hedge, walking in single file. Birdsong echoed around them, replacing the screech of the gulls. At one spot, walking into a deep cut-through in the hedge, the birds' twittering was so loud that any hope of conversation was lost.

"Your book didn't warn you about that, did it?" Mike shouted to Celeste. He frowned when she didn't respond.

"She can't hear you." Phoebe pointed at the fingers that Celeste had in her ears and Mike laughed. They passed through a gate and onto a quiet back road. It was lined on either side by a tall avenue of trees and would not have been out of place on the set of Game of Thrones. With more space to spread out, they naturally bunched into two groups; Celeste with Phoebe and Mike whilst, dawdling in their wake, Heather and Rita followed on with Eddie and Tolly.

"My friend got a pet beaver last week," Mike whispered to Phoebe. She looked at him over the top of Celeste's head. "He's called it Clint."

"And?" She eyed him suspiciously, waiting for the punchline.

"Clint Eatswood."

She swatted his arm with her hand, and he stuck his bottom lip out.

"You deserved that," she giggled, as Celeste suddenly pointed.

"Down here," she shouted, directing them to turn from the avenue and onto a narrow tarmac road. The sound altered as their boots hit the uniform asphalt and leading them on, Celeste started to march. The fence remained on their right-hand side, as they skirted the entire out of bounds area. Abruptly, after a further ten minutes of energetic marching, the barrier stopped and was replaced by a tightly packed line of portacabins. Narrow gaps between the moveable boxes allowed them to glimpse various machinery and materials accumulated on the other side; a pristine, yellow digger shone in the sunlight next to a huge heap of gravel and several cars were parked haphazardly, their tyres muddy from having driven across the field.

"Isn't Queen's Hill care home that way?" Heather shielded her eyes from the sun, as Tolly nodded in agreement. He swatted a fly away from his legs and peered through the fencing.

"I always thought I'd like to end up in there; such a beautiful location."

"Do you think they're developing the care home?"

"Maybe." Tolly turned three-hundred and sixty degrees. "That's over there, though, towards the Tower." On the left of the road, they could see the Manor, a large, imposing house, made from pale, weathered stone with turrets on all four corners. The compound seemed too far away to be for any work over there.

"I think there's going to be a development of warden assisted apartments," Phoebe offered as they continued to catch glimpses of the compound. Before anyone could reply, there was a sound from behind the portacabins of a car revving. It got louder, coming closer before it suddenly appeared near the entrance, gravel and mud being sprayed behind. With the group in the road, the car slowed to a halt as it waited for them to move to one side. Phoebe's heart sank. She recognized Thomas's ruddy face behind the wheel and, as he narrowed his eyes at her, she knew she'd been spotted. An electric motor sounded as the window slowly lowered.

"Fiona," he smirked, eyeing each of the Wanderers in turn.

"Phoebe," she corrected, deadpan.

"Right, yes." He tapped the side of his head. She tried not to glower at him; he must be doing it on purpose as no one's memory was *that* bad.

"You're wandering around here again?" He asked the question with the same smile she'd seen at work; it curled the lips but didn't reach any other part of his face.

"Just out for a walk Thomas. What about you?"

One of his eyes squinted and he paused, considering his response. "Just thought I'd check out the latest development." His pale blue eyes spotted the boxed drone being carried by Celeste. "Ah, we wondered where that had come from. Looking for anything in particular?"

Celeste pulled it closer to her body and tucked in behind her mum.

"We were investigating where the diversion would take us," Phoebe added, thinking on the spot.

"Anyone would think you were obsessed by that diversion," Thomas sneered, before covering it with a cough. He seemed edgy. "Well, you're nearly back to the path now, it's just around that corner." The window started to slide back up. "See you Monday." He continued to stare out until his window was fully up. Then he found first gear and drove off.

"He's a strange one; what's his problem?" Mike had been standing next to her the whole time. "Come on, don't let him spoil our walk." He squeezed her arm, and they moved off, following the direction pointed out by Thomas. As they rounded the bend, the view opened out before them. Phoebe's breath caught in her throat. It was magnificent, and the run in with her boss was immediately forgotten. One hundred and eighty degrees of brilliant, blue sea stood before them, glistening as the sun caught each ripple.

"They look like stars dancing," Celeste whispered. Phoebe nodded and for a moment they all watched in silence. Gundry's Tower was just visible to their right, tucked away; a solitary, elegant structure, now imprisoned behind ugly, unassailable metal fencing.

"Such a shame," Eddie joined her. "I've loved this view for years. Once upon a time there was a little café on the ground floor-"

"I remember that" Heather appeared and Phoebe budged to her left so the three of them could stand together.

"It used to sell squash in cups," Heather smiled at the memory and Phoebe realised they'd probably visited there about the same time.

"Did you ever go to the ice cream van?" Phoebe asked. "You could buy the most delicious vanilla cones." It was outside that café that she'd told her parents she was pregnant. She could almost taste that creamy ice cream now as she reminisced. After making the life changing announcement to her forgiving mum and dad she'd gone to buy everyone a cone; a tactical decision to give them time to consider the bombshell she'd just dropped. It had been just three weeks before they were due to start a new life in Spain and her announcement hadn't done anything to reduce the family's stress levels… talk about impeccable timing!

"Was there a man who put a second flake in your ice-cream, when his wife wasn't watching?" Heather's voice brought Phoebe back to the present, and she nodded.

"All the kids would hang around waiting… she must have known what was going on."

"Definitely," Heather agreed, "selling fifty ice-creams but getting through a hundred flakes!"

Everyone laughed and Phoebe was grateful she could still come here without it being tainted. After the initial shock at her news, her parents had rallied round and been a good support; her mum was overcome by the excitement of becoming a grandma while her dad had focused on the practical aspects of finances and needing a place to live, before they still jetted off to another country. The three women fell silent; caught in their memories of another time.

"Maybe it will open up again once the development is done." Eddie raised her eyebrows, looking hopeful but Phoebe shrugged. She wouldn't trust Thomas Johnson to look after anything, let alone preserve this special place and the memories it represented.

Chapter fifteen

With the drone packed away, the picnic eaten and coffee drunk, the Wanderers started their return journey. To complete a circular route rather than returning the way they'd come they had to follow a small track through a dense wood.

"I've never been this way before," Phoebe said. "We've always been able to walk along the footpath."

Mike agreed. "Me neither, but I've brought something to make the woods interesting for Celeste."

"Me?"

"And everyone else, if they want to join in."

Celeste still had energy for skipping but paused to wait patiently for Mike.

"I've heard there is treasure this way," he said mysteriously. Celeste caught her mum's eye, but Phoebe shrugged; she had no idea what he was talking about.

"Let me explain," he waved them both closer then with a grand flourish, produced a gadget from his pocket. It was about the size of a mobile phone, but more robust, coated in rubber. It looked as if it would bounce if dropped and proudly, he handed it to Celeste.

"This is a sat nav," he said, "do you know what that is?"

Celeste nodded and took the gadget. "We've one in the car."

"Right. But this one is like a treasure map. People have hidden their treasure and marked it on here. Anyone can download the map and use it to go on a treasure hunt." He waited for their reaction, looking between them. Now Phoebe remembered, *geo-caching*. He'd talked about it—or maybe it had been Rita—but she'd forgotten all about it until now. It sounded fun; she smiled at him, he'd obviously gone to a lot of effort to make sure Celeste wasn't bored on her day out.

"You see that path there?" He took the gadget back gently from Celeste and they both followed the direction he was pointing in.

"The track?"

The others bunched up to listen and Mike started to explain again. He had the patience of a saint!

"Geo-caching," he said louder, "I thought we could hunt for treasure." He received a mixed reception, and a loud tut from Tolly.

"I need you to direct us along there," he handed the device back to Celeste. "The marker will move as we move, to show where we are. You see that cross?"

Celeste nodded, her eyes hadn't left the machine in all the time he'd been talking.

"That is where the first treasure is hidden. Once we get near, instructions will pop up on screen, to give clues about the hiding place."

Celeste looked at Phoebe, waiting for her agreement to go ahead.

"You be careful with it-"

"I will—promise." Celeste wrapped both hands around the machine and waited for everyone to fall in line behind. "Let's go." They moved off in single file, looking around as if going on a bear hunt. Celeste guided them along the path, following the marker silently while Phoebe and Mike trotted closely behind. For ten minutes the only sound was their feet tramping along the path. A low stone wall to the left marked the edge of the field beyond, when suddenly Celeste stopped.

"Woah." Phoebe narrowly avoided crashing into her.

"Look!" Celeste spun round and held the gadget up for Mike to see.

"What does it say?" He drew level and motioned for her to read it, as the others caught up.

"What's happening?" Rita appeared, her cheeks ruddy from the exercise.

Celeste held out the sat nav. "That cross marks where treasure is hidden."

"Treasure?" Rita turned to Mike who nodded enthusiastically in return.

"The Brownies would love this, Brown Owl." Celeste grinned at her while they waited for the back markers of the group. "Look," she hopped up and down excitedly as the screen updated, "there's a clue now."

"Can you read it out for everyone?" Mike beckoned the adults to gather round.

"Look to the left, along the wall," Celeste glanced up, her eyes shining. "Walk to the gate and you'll see it all." Her eyes looked off into the distance. "There! 'Walk to the gate'" she repeated, pointing to a sturdy wooden structure in the wall. "Come on," she started to run towards it.

"You heard the lady," Mike shouted, "come on." He grabbed Phoebe's hand and, caught up in the excitement, she ran with him. At the wall, they spread out, searching. Phoebe's eyes roved around the stones. They were neat, uniform and in good repair. She stepped to the right, looking methodically along the stones, before stepping again. She glanced over. Mike, and Celeste, were both engrossed, looking at the wall and all the others had fanned out, their eyes searching among the stones. As if sensing her, Mike glanced over and smiled. She held his gaze, feeling her heart lift; then he broke eye contact and pointed. Mid-way between them something looked out of place. They stepped towards it, and he waved her on to investigate. Phoebe peered closer then shrieked. A box was lodged between two stones.

"Celeste! Celeste!"

The little girl turned and began running at full pelt towards them. "What is it?"

"There. You look."

She closed in then spotted it, catching her breath in excitement as she pulled the green plastic box out from its hiding place. She waved it in the air, showing the others.

"Open it." Phoebe was equally as excited.

Celeste pulled the lid off and looked inside as Mike explained the rules; she could take one item as a keepsake if she replaced it with something they'd brought. Her face fell and she turned to her mum.

"We didn't bring anything, did we?"

Oh no, she'd totally forgotten. Phoebe patted her pockets, wondering what she had with her that they could use, when Mike held out his hand. Nestled in his palm was a small metallic compass, a pink fridge magnet and a miniature box of playing cards.

"Christmas crackers," he said sheepishly, "but perfect for this sort of thing." Celeste's mouth formed a large 'O'. Happy she now had something to leave, she moved the treasure with her finger, thoughtfully considering each item. Finally, she took out an orange-haired troll and in its place, she squeezed in the playing cards.

"She loves trolls," Phoebe whispered, stroking her daughter's hair lovingly while Celeste did the exact same thing to the troll's.

"Maybe there'll be a troll in the next box; if you are up for finding another?" As Celeste shrieked her response Mike held his hands over his ears, pretending to be deafened by her excited noise.

Mike pulled his car up outside Phoebe's house and turned the engine off. While Phoebe and Celeste had got a lift back with Rita, he'd done a detour to pick up fish and chips; the smell of the takeaway hung thick in the air and Mike's stomach gave a loud growl. He was starving. As he bent to retrieve the warm bag from the passenger footwell, the front door of the house flew open and Celeste appeared, waving him in.

"We've got everything ready," she shouted, "come on." He locked the car and the metal gate squeaked as he pushed through it. A movement to his right made him look and a pensioner was standing in the window watching. Celeste spotted her and waved, the older woman's face lighting up when she spotted her neighbour.

"Fish and chips," Celeste shouted, pointing to the bag in Mike's hand. She rubbed circles on her stomach. The window swung open, and the woman leaned out.

"Did you have a good day?" She peered at Celeste.

"It was fab," Celeste hopped on the path, "and this is Mike."

Feeling suddenly self-conscious, he waved. "Hello, pleased to meet you. I'm bringing supplies," he waved the bag. "We're back much later than we'd expected."

"Nice to meet you, Mike. I'm Agnes." She paused, peering at him through her glasses. "Have we met before?"

Mike took a step back, surprised. He shook his head. "No, I don't think so."

"Hmm, you look awfully familiar."

Phoebe appeared in the doorway, looking to see what the commotion was about. She smiled at her neighbour, "who looks familiar?"

Agnes tapped her chin, squinting as she continued to scrutinize Mike.

"This is Mike." Phoebe touched his arm, and he felt her warmth through his jumper.

"Yes. I'm trying to remember where I know him from."

"Oh?" Phoebe frowned, "you two know each other?"

"I don't think so."

"Don't listen to me, I must be mistaken." Agnes shook her head and flashed a smile at them. "I understand he's bringing your tea."

"He is. Would you like to come over? I could do you a chip butty?"

"Oh no love. I'll leave you to it. Celebrity Catchphrase is on in a minute. I love Stephen Mulhern. I remember when…" she paused and rolled her eyes. "Listen to me nattering on. You go and get your tea before it gets cold."

"You sure? Come over for lunch tomorrow, I'll do a roast chicken. One o'clock?"

"Lovely. You can tell me all about today."

"Good luck trying to get Celeste to talk about anything *other* than today," Phoebe laughed, as she went back in the house and held the door for the others to join her.

"Nice to meet you," Mike waved, keeping his head slightly turned, as he stepped over the threshold.

"You too love," Agnes squinted as he disappeared. "You *do* remind me of someone though," she whispered.

The plates had been cleared away and Celeste was upstairs getting ready for bed. Sitting at the table, Phoebe and Mike nursed cups of tea and Mike now knew all about Agnes and her beloved Bert, both of whom had been like parents to Phoebe for the last ten years.

"I told my mum and dad about Celeste at Gundry's Tower." Phoebe absent mindedly stirred her cup even though most of the tea had been drunk. "They'd just sold their house as they were moving to Spain, and time was running out. I needed to decide whether to move with them or stay here with Eric, my boyfriend. Then I found out I was pregnant, and everything changed." She paused, clearly back at that difficult moment in her life.

"What happened next?"

"I decided to stay. I bought this house and Eric moved in with me." She paused and stared at the spoon. "That was a mistake."

"What, staying?"

"No. Eric." She looked at Mike. "He stayed a few months, then moved back with his mum."

"I'm sorry Phoebe," he put his hand over hers. "Is he still involved now?"

Phoebe shrugged. "He's okay when he's around. At first he helped quite a bit, his mum did too. But when Celeste was nearly two Marie, his mum, died. It was sudden, unexpected and it hit Eric hard. He needed a fresh start, so he moved to London."

"How did you cope?"

Phoebe shrugged. "I just got on with it. Agnes and Bert were great. I think I'd probably have moved to Spain otherwise."

"I'm glad you didn't."

She smiled at him, and he realised what a strong person she really was. Beneath the polka dots and the red lipstick, she was made of real grit.

"Eric sends some money, remembers her birthday," she sniffed. "We went for a weekend to London, and he met up with us. We spent a day seeing the sights and he treated us; it was nice. I can't complain."

"Well, he's the one missing out and you're doing an amazing job. Celeste seems happy." A loud thud came from upstairs, making them both look up.

"Ha, you won't be saying that when she comes through the ceiling."

Mike took Phoebe's hand and raised it to his lips. He gently kissed it and held her gaze.

"Mum! Come on!" Celeste's voice shouted impatiently down the stairs and Mike released Phoebe's hand, nodding towards the hallway.

"Go on. I'll wash up while you sort her out. Then I'd better get going; I should leave you to it."

Phoebe stood and walked round to his side of the table. Taking his face in her hands she bent down and slowly kissed his lips. A spark of electricity shot through his body, and he opened his eyes to find her watching him intently.

"Thank you for today, Mike," she whispered, "we've both had a wonderful time."

"Me too," he managed, his voice hoarse. He watched her walk out the room and sighed, before collecting the dishes and taking them to the sink. He turned on the tap, pausing while the water warmed up. It was nice being in a house where other people were; he could hear the clatter upstairs as they moved around. He ran his fingers under the tap; he really needed to get home and catch up with some work, but the thought of leaving them made his spirits sink.

Chapter Sixteen

As soon as the doorbell rang at one o'clock, Celeste barrelled down the hallway to be the first to open the front door.

"Oomph love."

Celeste threw her arms around her neighbour for a hug and Agnes took a step backwards to steady herself. Phoebe arrived from the kitchen.

"Celeste. Be careful."

Agnes waved it away. "She's alright. I'm not that doddery—yet," she added as she chucked Celeste under the chin with her finger. Phoebe beckoned her neighbour in.

"Come through, come through," she called nipping back to the kitchen. "Celeste, hang her coat up."

Agnes joined her in the kitchen, watching patiently while Phoebe opened the oven door to check on the roast potatoes.

"Is Mike here?"

Phoebe glanced up. "No; were you expecting him to be?"

"I just wondered if he was staying for lunch?"

Phoebe pushed the tray of potatoes back in the oven and closed the door. She blew on her face, trying to get the curls away from her eyes, then narrowed them at her neighbour.

"*Staying* for lunch? He went home last night, after the fish and chips."

"Oh, did he?" Did Agnes sound disappointed? Phoebe watched her pick at some imaginary fluff on her cardigan before she looked up and smiled.

"You are naughty, Agnes."

"Do you not fancy him, love?"

"Agnes!" Phoebe lowered her voice then checking the door, sat down opposite her neighbour. "He's really nice, isn't he?" She giggled and Agnes patted her hand. "He's going to ring me later, but we had a lovely day yesterday, and Celeste hasn't stopped talking about him."

Agnes squeezed her hand. "I'm so pleased for you love. He does seem very nice, although he looks *so* familiar. Where does he work…oh, never mind?"

"We're just taking things slowly; I've got Celeste to think about."

"Very sensible, but I'm happy to babysit anytime, you know that."

The buzzer sounded on the oven and Phoebe grabbed the oven gloves, taking a sizzling chicken out and putting it on the side to cool.

"Love, you didn't need to go to all this trouble," Agnes said, her eyes roving around the kitchen and taking in a tray of Yorkshire puddings and the pan full of vegetables. Phoebe puffed up with pride. If there was one thing she was good at, it was cooking an excellent roast dinner. And it was the least she could do, for abandoning her neighbour so much over the last few days.

"It's no bother." Phoebe moved to the fridge. "And look what I've made… especially for you." She presented a glass bowl full of trifle. "Your favourite, I do believe."

"Oh love," Agnes's hands flew up to her face. "What have I done to deserve this; it's not my birthday?" She joked, but Phoebe noticed her wipe some moisture from her eyes.

"Totally selfish on my part," Phoebe laughed. "I need to make sure you've got enough energy for this week's school pick-ups."

Agnes had been looking even more bird-like than normal, she'd only weigh five stone soaking wet, and the guilt of not popping in to see her more frequently, mixed with a low level of constant worry, meant Phoebe needed to check she was looking after herself. "I've made far too much trifle; you're going to be eating it for days. I'll give you a box to take back next door."

"I won't say no," Agnes chuckled, easing off her cardigan as the warmth of the kitchen enveloped her. "So how was yesterday, anyway?"

Phoebe relaxed and told her about meeting the other Wanderers and their leisurely walk. Agnes listened patiently as she detailed the footpath, and the stunning scenery.

"But what about Mike? He seems like a keeper."

Phoebe smiled coyly. "He was the perfect gent the whole day; we couldn't have asked for anyone nicer."

"But?"

Phoebe raised her eyebrows. "But nothing."

"You sound like there's a problem."

"No. No problem." Phoebe shook her head, turning off the oven and picking up the three plates that had been warming on top of the hob. "He's lovely. I'm just… taking it slow."

"Why?"

"Gosh," Phoebe laughed as she started to dish out vegetables, "is this the Spanish inquisition?"

"I know you, young lady; there's something you're not telling me."

"There's not, I'm just taking it slow."

"Don't take it too slow."

"Agnes!" Phoebe pretended to be shocked. "We've literally had one date."

"Good men don't hang around for long, that's all I'm saying." Agnes eyed the dishes that lay around the kitchen counters. "Can I help you with anything?"

Phoebe shook her head and raised her head to the ceiling. "Celeste! Dinner!"

They heard the thud as Celeste jumped off her bed and ran across her room. The two women paused, looking at each other.

"I know Eric left you in the lurch," Agnes spoke quietly, "but you were both so young, you were just kids."

Phoebe nodded; it was true. A lot of water had flowed under the bridge since then.

"But don't push everyone away because of one bad experience." Agnes took a tissue out of her sleeve and blew her nose. "For what it's worth, I thought he seemed really lovely," she said brightly. "But if he messes you about, I'll give him a piece of my mind. No one messes with my girls."

Phoebe laughed and wrapped an oven-gloved arm around her friend. "What would I do without you?"

"You'd struggle, that's true," Agnes said, pretending to be serious. "So will you give him another go?"

"Maybe."

"Go on, see him again."

Celeste ran into the room and skidded across the kitchen tiles in her socks. "Who are you seeing again?"

"Big ears! We were just talking about Mike and the Wanderers."

"It was brilliant. We had so much fun. Eddie and Tolly helped me tick things off in my I-Spy books." She skidded back out the room before returning carrying her four books. "Look!" She flicked through the pages, stopping occasionally to point out the animals or flowers that she'd spotted on the walk. "Tolly kept giving me mints which were chewy in the middle." She took a plate from her mum and put it on her placemat. "Yum-my." She picked up a Yorkshire pudding and started to nibble its edges. "Brown Owl and Heather did the route too; maybe I could help Mike plan it next time. I could get my map reading badge." Having exhausted her conversation, she sat down properly on her chair and waited for her mum to sit. They all started to eat.

"Did you like Mike?"

Phoebe frowned at Agnes, urging caution. What was she playing at? But Celeste laughed, nodding her head enthusiastically.

"He was so funny," she shovelled a chunk of carrot into her mouth.

"Celeste. Don't talk with your mouth full."

She chewed quickly then swallowed, opening her mouth to show her mum it was empty. "He was great. He brought a drone and let me fly it-"

"Really?" Agnes leant in, keen to keep the girl talking.

"-uh-huh. He'd made it, he said. Even Tolly thought it was good and he didn't say that much; particularly with Mike." Celeste shrugged and loaded her fork up with more roast dinner. "But they're all friends, aren't they, mama?"

Before Phoebe could finish her mouthful and agree, Agnes carried on, keen to get more information out of Celeste.

"So, this drone-"

Phoebe frowned but Agnes lifted her shoulders as if to ask what her problem was.

"-he let you fly it, you say. What did you see?"

Phoebe quietly ate her dinner. It was nice to hear Celeste so animated about her day out. Every time Celeste mentioned Mike by name Phoebe noticed that Agnes raised her eyebrows slightly.

"Okay Celeste," Phoebe interrupted once she'd finished most of her food. "Come on now, finish your lunch before it gets cold."

Celeste nodded and loaded more food into her mouth while the two women ate quietly, happy in each other's company. As Agnes put her knife and fork together, she rubbed her stomach. "That was lovely. Thank you so much."

"You're welcome." Phoebe topped up the glasses with wine, a nice Sauvignon Blanc that she knew Agnes wouldn't object to, even though it was white wine. She took a sip and relaxed, knowing her neighbour had eaten a good portion, and if she could get her to have trifle too, even better.

"I had an interesting day yesterday too." Agnes took a drink and placed her glass gently back on the table.

Phoebe narrowed her eyes, intrigued. "Oh? What did you get up to?" She turned her full attention on her neighbour.

"You know I've been thinking about how much longer I'll be able to stay in that house?"

"Um." Phoebe was now fully alert. Agnes had mentioned about the house being too big for her several times over the past years, but nothing more had ever happened. Phoebe glanced at Celeste; she was only half listening, her eyes on her I-Spy books while she finished her lunch.

"I had Ben from the Estate Agents round."

"What?" Phoebe leaned forward, elbows on the table. "You didn't tell me you'd planned that."

"I didn't want you to fuss, love. I needed to know how much he thought I could sell it for, *if* I wanted to," she added, with emphasis. "I didn't want to get you all stressed for nothing, if it's only worth a few bob."

"Well?"

"I'm getting to that." She smiled and waved her hand as if to calm her. "I was shocked, I'd get a tidy sum. It would mean I could buy a lovely little flat in town-"

"In town?" Phoebe put her hand on Agnes's arm, her heart sinking at the thought of her friend, and support system, moving away.

"-I wouldn't go far, and I'll still help with my lovely girl, collecting from school, as now."

Celeste looked up from her books and grinned; the enormity of the changes that might be coming their way were totally lost on her. Phoebe gently stroked her daughter's hair, surprised that Agnes had gone ahead with the visit, without telling her. But then, she hadn't spent much time with her neighbour over the last week, and guilt settled on her shoulders.

Had she been neglecting her? Perhaps she'd been too caught up with work, Mike, the Tower, the Wanderers… the list went on.

"I'm sorry love," Agnes patted her hand. "I know it's a shock for you, but I've realised that sometimes you need to do what's right for *you*, or me, in this case."

Phoebe nodded; she got it, but it didn't make it any easier when she thought about Agnes moving away.

"I'm so relieved I've told you." Agnes clasped her hands and looked up to the ceiling. "I hated being secretive. I kept thinking you were going to come back early and catch me out. It's much better to be upfront, isn't it?" She sipped her wine, looking serious. "I don't want you to think it's about the money, although think how many holidays we could have," she chuckled. "It's more about keeping on top of the house; it's far too big for one person and it's a waste really. Some nice family could do much more with the space than me." Agnes paused and Phoebe put her hand on her arm to still her.

"It's fine, Agnes, we'll work it all out. I'm just sorry you felt you had to keep it secret, that must have been stressful for you."

As the two women stood to embrace, Celeste joined in and wrapped her little arms around the outside of them both. Phoebe closed her eyes and savoured the moment, but something niggled at her. She thought about her own situation and how she was creeping around at work. She was being secretive too, and it was making her uneasy. In that moment, spurred on by Agnes's honesty, she determined to be upfront. She was going to find a moment to speak to Thomas at the office tomorrow and to ask him, once and for all, what exactly was going on at Gundry's Tower.

Chapter Seventeen

Monday morning and Phoebe had it all under control. They had eaten breakfast, were dressed and ready to leave the house when the letterbox snapped on the front door. Several envelopes fell to the floor and, while Celeste slowly slid her feet into her school shoes, Phoebe flicked through the post. The early good vibes disappeared as she pulled out a letter; typed in bold red font it read 'Account Overdue'. Her eyes dropped to the box at the end of the page, containing the amount. She sighed. Four hundred pounds. She'd have to phone them and ask for a delay in paying as it was still another week until payday. That promotion would really have helped. She shoved the envelope in her bag and resolved to start another job search as soon as she got a free moment. She locked the door behind them and got in the car. Once she was sure that Celeste was belted in, she turned the ignition. Nothing happened. The last remaining good vibe bubble now popped and disappeared into the ether. How could such a positive start to the day go downhill so quickly? She glanced over to see Agnes watching from her window; occasionally their exit in the morning coincided with Agnes opening her curtains and, if it did, they always exchanged a brief wave. Now Phoebe grimaced at her and shrugged her shoulders. She tried the ignition again. Nothing. Her mobile rang and, wondering how Agnes had got to her phone so quickly, she was surprised to see Mike's name light up on screen.

"Morning," he sounded full of beans. "I thought I'd give you a quick bell before you headed off to work. How are both this morning?"

"Good thanks, how are you?" She mentally kicked herself; she wasn't good, she was stressing.

"All good, yes."

The line crackled and she could make out background noise. "Are you in the car?"

"I am," he raised his voice. "Just heading near yours actually. I made an early start and picked up some supplies from town. Thought I'd give you a call as there's something I've been meaning to mention-"

"Near mine?"

"Yes, I'll be passing in two minutes. Have you time for a quick coffee and a chat?"

"I'd love to, but unfortunately I don't have the time," she paused. "Actually, I wonder whether you could help us out." She explained her predicament. A minute later they got out the car and were heading back up the path when Agnes opened her front door. She waved a tenner at them.

"Want me to call you a taxi?"

Phoebe shook her head. "There's no need," she smiled. The toot of a horn made them look to the road, as Mike's sleek Range Rover pulled up behind her old banger.

"Mike?" Agnes took a step down her drive, her fluffy pink slippers incongruous against the jet-black tarmac. "How did he get here so quickly?"

"He was passing," Phoebe whispered, watching as Mike hopped out and waved.

"That was handy," Agnes said quietly, nudging Phoebe's arm.

"Wasn't it just. Perhaps the day isn't going to be so bad after all." Phoebe kissed the older woman's soft cheek. "See you later." Celeste hopped about on the pavement, chatting to Mike and he dropped a light kiss on Phoebe's cheek as she joined them.

"Hi Agnes, lovely day." He pointed up to the sun, which was already warm and burning off the overnight dew.

"Certainly is," she squinted at him, looking at his face. "Might get out in the garden later."

"I'll help you tonight if you want to plant those seeds out," Phoebe paused getting in the car, but Agnes waved her away.

"I'll see how much I can do. You enjoy yourselves, go on, don't be late." She gave a last wave then shuffled back indoors.

"I don't know what she thinks we're up to," Phoebe laughed, "but I certainly won't be enjoying myself for the next eight hours." She helped Celeste into the back seat but, despite her words, she was back to her optimistic self from that morning. She would have to call the garage and no doubt face a daunting bill to get her car on the road again, but she pushed that thought to the back of her mind and enjoyed being driven to Celeste's school. After a hasty goodbye, ushering her daughter in through the gate, they continued to the Council offices. She gathered her bag from the footwell, the car's low hum filling the vehicle as it idled by the kerb. She breathed in the smell of the leather interior and ran her hand over the seat—she could get used to this luxury—then checked herself, an image of her own banger flitting into her mind. She couldn't get caught up in this fairy tale.

"Thanks Mike," she clutched her bag, smiling at him. "You got me out of a spot just now."

"My pleasure, glad I could help." He held her gaze, seeming in no rush to get back to wherever he was headed. "Might you be in town at lunch?"

She shook her head. She'd got lunch in her bag, sandwiches she'd made the night before. She normally brought in lunch, having to keep an eye on the pennies meant she didn't normally go out to eat. "I'll probably stay at work, to be honest."

He nodded. "I just wondered when I might be able to see you again?"

Her insides melted as she mentally ran through her diary. She'd really like to see him soon.

"Tomorrow evening?" He suggested.

"I can't tomorrow, sorry. Celeste has a ballet concert. She's been working towards it for weeks."

"Where is it?"

"At St. Luke's church, in town."

"How will you get there?"

She paused. She hadn't thought about that yet, particularly now she might be carless.

"I could give you a lift."

"You don't need to do that."

"I'd like to; can't have her catching the bus in her tutu." They laughed. Her eyes fell to his mouth; when resting his lips curled up at the ends, making him look like he had a slight smile even when being serious. *Don't go too slow*, Agnes had said.

"Phoebe?"

"Yes, I'd like that, thanks."

"In fact, could I come in and watch," he said, adding, "would that be alright? Do I need to buy a ticket?"

Phoebe laughed at his enthusiasm. "Are you sure?" She looked around, then whispered, "it's not exactly the Bolshoi you know."

Now it was his turn to chuckle. "Maybe not, but there are worse ways to pass an hour or two." He leant in, "besides, it'll save me driving home and then coming back to collect you."

She shrugged. She thought he was mad but equally, if it meant she could see him again, and get a lift both ways then great. Win-win situation.

"If you're sure, that would be really good."

As she walked into work, she had a spring in her step, happy that her personal life was finally on the up. It was about time her luck began to change and now, she wondered if her work life could follow.

Phoebe was determined to find out more information about Gundry's Tower and, with no time like the present, she swung left into the admin office. It was empty, no one there. Her heart started to pick up speed as she approached Thomas's office and knocked on the door. With her shoulders back, she looked much more confident than she felt. No response. She gingerly pushed open the door.

"Hello, anyone around?" She was about to back out when she noticed a pile of buff-coloured files on Thomas's desk. Curiosity got the better of her. Had he been lying about the paperwork? It certainly hadn't been in Archives as he'd suggested. She crossed the floor and flicked through. 'Guycliffe Manor house', 'Manor Road development', 'St. Katherine's Community Hall'—all names she recognised, "Gundry's Tower". A-ha! He'd had it all along. She pulled it out from the pile and placed it on the desk, letting her bags fall to the floor. The question was, had he known it was there and lied, or had he genuinely thought it was finished with? That rather depended on what was in the file. She opened it. A letter from the Ramblers Association:

> *'Dear Sir, Following the recent planning permission approval for Carpenter Construction to develop assisted living accommodation at Queen's Hill care home (site of Gundry's Tower) we would like to register our strongest objection to this approval. We fully intend to submit through the appeals process....'*

She flicked to the next document. Her heart sank. It was a planning survey report. 'Aurelius', she didn't recognise them as a consultancy firm that the Council had used before. She frowned and scanned the report.

> *'No reason to suspect that the development would damage any of the flora in the area.'*

She huffed; *anyone* could see that it would do irreparable damage. A noise behind made her turn. Thomas stood in the doorway; his mouth dropped open as he took in the scene in front of him. She gulped; this probably didn't look good.

"I-" she stammered.

"You! What on earth are you doing in my office?"

She closed the file and shoved it back onto the pile. Her cheeks flamed red as her brain racked for something to say.

"I was looking for the Gun-"

"Don't tell me-" he interrupted holding his hands up, "Gundry's Tower." He crossed the office and slammed his hand down on the pile of folders. "What is your obsession with that place?"

"It's no obsession, Thomas," she whispered, then took a deep breath; a chill ran through her as she met his eyes. He looked livid.

"It's no obsession, Thomas. I just want to find out the truth about what is happening there."

"The truth. You make it sound like there is something sinister at play."

"The documents were not in Archives like you said-"

"Well," he was taken aback by the directness of her words, "I can't be expected to know where *all* the paperwork is, for *every* development."

"But you seem to be… obstructing my enquiries."

He laughed and took a step forward. He was a big man, and she shrank back, conscious that it was just the two of them. She had no support and there'd be no witnesses to whatever was about to happen.

"Just *who* do you think you are, Phoebe?" He spoke very quietly, with menace. "'Obstructing your enquiries' indeed." He made air quotes, then let his hands drop. "Planning permission was granted. There was an appeal. It was turned down. Work is starting soon-"

"But why is there no public record of all of this? Why can't I find the appeal notes?"

"Why should you? It's not one of your cases."

"But as a matter of public record, you know it should be fully documented and available."

"You are really overstepping the mark here. I've already warned you, yet you seem intent on trying to provoke me at every opportunity." He sniffed then took a step back. Calmly he removed his coat and hung it on a peg, marking his territory. He walked round his desk and sat down. He switched on his computer and tapped in his password, waiting for it to boot up. He appeared to be the opposite of Phoebe, whose knees were now trembling as the adrenalin rush hit her system. Unsure what to do, she picked up her bags; the movement made Thomas look up.

"I suggest you go to your office; I need to consider what to do next."

"What do you mean?" She whispered; the wind now gone from her sails. Thomas merely pointed to the door.

"If you've any sense you'll get out of my office now," he said calmly, turning to his computer.

"But Thomas-"

"Go. I need to think."

She walked out and closed the door behind her. That had turned very weird, but she doubted that would be the end of it; he surely had something else up his sleeve. A wave of anxiety washed over her, but she heeded his advice and ran down the corridor. A heavy feeling settled in the pit of her stomach as anxiously she wondered what exactly he was now thinking about.

Phoebe had her head over a document, pretending to be hard at work. The words were swimming in front of her eyes, and she'd been staring at the same page for several minutes. Penny had made her a coffee, but hadn't interrupted, assuming she'd got in early to do some work. A shadow passed over the document and Phoebe looked up.

Thomas stood at the end of her desk, his stomach resting against it as he gave a tight smile.

"Phoebe. I wonder if I could have a word—in my office, please?" Without waiting for a response, he turned and left. Phoebe's heart started to pound. She wiped her sweating hands on her skirt as she stood up.

"What's he want you for?" Penny appeared over the desk divider.

Phoebe shrugged, "I've no idea," she lied. She hastened along the corridor and into the admin office. His assistant looked up and pointed to the door.

"He said to go straight through."

Phoebe knocked once and went in, closing the door behind her. There were two people in the room; Thomas was back in his swivel chair but was turned to face a short woman who stood by his side. She wore a sombre navy skirt and jacket; a white blouse was buttoned up to her chin and her hair was scraped back in a tight bun. Phoebe recognised her—Evelyn, their HR Manager—and her stomach sank. This couldn't be good. Thomas, his face neutral, waved Phoebe to approach his desk, and indicated the chair opposite. As she took a seat, she tried to swallow but nothing happened, her mouth devoid of any moisture.

"Phoebe, I called Evelyn to explain the situation I found myself in this morning."

Phoebe nodded. Thomas turned to Evelyn, who cleared her throat.

"Phoebe, having heard Thomas's concerns about your recent behaviour I believe that we have no option but to suspend you from work, pending a disciplinary investigation."

"What?" Phoebe leant forwards.

Evelyn raised her hand, and continued, "You'll be suspended on full pay while we investigate. We discussed keeping you at work however due to the nature of the allegations we don't feel it is appropriate for you to remain in the building, with colleagues. We will conduct our investigations as quickly as we can, and you'll receive a letter shortly from us to explain what will happen next, together with the exact nature of the allegations against you." She paused, satisfied that she'd almost reached the end of her speech without any further interruptions. "You must not contact any colleagues while you are suspended. You must not try to access the building, your emails or computer files. Do you have any questions?"

"Um." Phoebe's head was spinning; she concentrated on breathing. "Er, what exactly am I being suspended for?"

"That will be outlined in the letter we'll send to you, Phoebe." Evelyn glanced at Thomas then down to her notepad. "At the moment, the allegations include insubordination and ignoring management advice."

Phoebe stared at her, reeling. 'Insubordination?'

Evelyn nodded once then pointed towards the door. "Now if you are ready, Phoebe, we'll gather your personal belongings and then I have to escort you off the premises." She nodded at the lanyard around Phoebe's neck. "I'll also need to take your ID pass I'm afraid, for the period of suspension."

Chapter Eighteen

Phoebe walked home slowly; words and thoughts jumbling around her head as she replayed and replayed the various scenes that had led to this point. She trudged along the High Street, everywhere evoking memories; the camping shop made her think of Amir and Sadiq, and therefore Rita and the weekend with the Brownies. The steamy café where she'd met up with Mike; the Woodpecker Inn where she'd first met him. So much had happened within a few weeks and she couldn't help equating her current dire situation with Mike, the Wanderers and Gundry's Tower. On autopilot, she turned into her road. Her feet knew where to go to carry her home and it was a relief not to have to make any decisions. She walked up her path and opened her handbag for her keys. She felt around the inside, her eyes beginning to swim with tears at the thought of locking herself away inside. She roughly wiped at her eyes and felt for the lock on the door. It was only as she fumbled with the key that she became aware of a voice shouting.

"Phoebe! Love, are you okay? I was shouting." Agnes hurried up the path in her wellies, a gardening trowel in hand. She stopped, her mouth dropping as Phoebe turned to her. "Phoebe love, what on earth is the matter?" Agnes almost ran up the path and managed to catch Phoebe before she crumpled to the floor.

"Is Celeste okay? You okay?"

Phoebe nodded. "Everyone's okay." She heard Agnes sigh with relief.

"Come on then, let's get you in and you can tell me what's going on."

Agnes put a tray down on the whitewashed coffee table in Phoebe's living room.

"Come on love, you need to keep your strength up." She handed the younger woman a plate with a ham sandwich, then nudged a mug of tea towards her.

"From what you've told me you haven't really done anything wrong," she added, narrowing her eyes. "The only thing he can complain about is that you were in his office, looking through the files."

Phoebe groaned.

"But that should just be a telling off. Are you in a Union?"

Phoebe shook her head.

"Hmmph." Agnes sipped her mug of tea. "It sounds like he's got an axe to grind if you ask me; I wonder why. You haven't had a run in with him before, have you?"

Again, Phoebe shook her head, then paused in nibbling the edge of a sandwich. "Well, apart from us both going for the same job."

"Does he know you went for his job?"

Phoebe nodded, chewing a mouthful of bread. "He was also on the panel for the last interview, and obviously didn't think I was up to doing that either."

Agnes narrowed her eyes. "Maybe he feels threatened by you; sees you as the competition?"

Phoebe shrugged and pulled a face. She didn't understand why if that was the case.

"I wonder if Rita might be able to help you," Agnes suggested. "I used to be good at the office politics when Bert was alive, I helped him out with all sorts, you wouldn't believe," she sniffed. "But I'm a bit," she made quote marks in the air, "'out the loop' now."

Phoebe smiled gratefully at her neighbour. "I don't believe you could ever be 'out the loop'" she made the same gesture back to her neighbour. "You always provide very good counsel." They sat quietly, contemplating the events that were taking place.

"If they call you in for a meeting-"

Phoebe tutted. "*When* they call me in."

"- well, you should be able to take someone with you into the meeting."

"But I'm not allowed to speak to any colleagues."

"Rita isn't employed there; and she's your friend rather than a colleague."

"She's still involved with them; I don't want to give them any more ammunition. I certainly don't want to put her in an awkward position."

"What about Mike then?"

Phoebe shook her head, a frown appearing on her forehead. "No way," she said. She hadn't worked out her feelings about him yet. "It's because of him I'm in this mess."

"Oh now, that's not really fair-"

"If Mike hadn't asked, I wouldn't have been looking for information about Gundry's."

"-that's not strictly true, is it?"

"It is."

"But I thought it stopped you and the Brownies from getting to the Tower last weekend. Wouldn't you or Rita have been curious, done some digging of your own?"

Phoebe shrugged. "Probably not."

Agnes snorted. "I think you would. And, if not you, then Rita wouldn't have ignored it."

"But Rita's not the one who's about to lose her job, is she?" Phoebe mechanically chewed on her sandwich as her eyes began to fill with tears.

Agnes tutted and patted her hand. "Come on now. It won't come to that, love."

"I can't lose my job Agnes," Phoebe whispered, "I just can't. I've got no savings, I've got the mortgage to pay, plus now the bloody car—oh," her eyes filled even more, "and I forgot, a credit card bill."

Agnes leaned over and pulled Phoebe towards her. "You'll get through this, love. I just wish I could help more." She kissed her on the cheek then glanced at her slim wristwatch. "Look now, it's nearly three o'clock. Do you want me to get Celeste as normal, and take her back to mine? You get yourself sorted." She stood and collected the empty cups then paused by the door. "Why don't you write down what you can remember about all of this; dates, who said what. Just some notes in case you have to go and explain yourself. Come to mine when you're ready, and I'll cook tea for us tonight."

"You don't need to-"

"Oh shush," said the older woman, mock annoyed. "Stop being so independent. Let others help-"

"But I can-"

"- I *know* you can," Agnes said firmly, "but let me help you today." She paused, looking thoughtful. "Are you going to tell Celeste?"

Phoebe shook her head. Her little girl was a born worrier and Phoebe didn't need to fuel that fire just yet. "No, not until it's sorted. I'll tell her I've got a few days of holiday to use if she asks."

"You've been talking about painting the shed for ages," Agnes suggested. "It might keep you busy; stop you dwelling on things."

Whilst it was the last thing Phoebe felt like doing, she always liked to use her time productively and she would need to keep busy to stop her mind from working overtime. "Thanks Agnes. Just pretend I'm still at work and I'll come round in a couple of hours. I'll take Celeste to school tomorrow though—let you have a lie in."

"That's a deal." Agnes rose to her feet and patted Phoebe's arm. "Don't worry love," she gave it a squeeze, "it'll be alright." She held Phoebe's eye for a moment then looked at the wellies in the hallway.

"Look at that," she pointed to them. "I'd better nip home and get my shoes; I can't really turn up at the school gates in those now, can I? See you later, lovey."

"Thanks Agnes." Phoebe followed her down the hallway and saw her out. She smiled as Agnes walked up her own driveway, then she turned her back and shut the door, finally blocking out the world. She paused to look at herself in the gold-framed hall mirror, then sank to the floor and allowed the tears to fall. How could she have been so stupid? Everything she'd worked so hard to build over the last decade was now on a knife-edge. She'd been persuaded by a man *again* and, just like before, trouble had followed close behind. Now, just like last time, she was the one who would have to face the consequences.

Chapter Nineteen

Tolly sat quietly reading his book. He had manoeuvred his camping chair into a patch of sunlight, next to the tents, and was enjoying the peace now Heather had gone to her tent. He closed his book and looked around at the distant hills. The site was arranged over several fields, each neatly hedged with bushes to provide screening and privacy for the many pitches. Large trees were dotted around the whole area, giving shade. They had spared no expense in maintaining a country feel to the place. Tolly sighed and tapped his book. He couldn't concentrate. Eddie had gone for a walk, and he half expected his mobile to ring with the next request or emergency. Life was never quiet when the Maguires were around. He shut his eyes, the sun was warm on his face, and he had a dull ache in his legs from their bike ride that morning. It had been a disaster; they'd argued, got lost and found that the only pub for miles around was closed for the day. Worse, Heather had had an accident, hitting a pigeon and falling off her bike on the way home. She was now sulking and nursing a swollen face. Relations weren't good between the three of them at the moment. He sat, enjoying five minutes of quiet before the sound of an approaching car made him open his eyes to investigate. He recognized Mike's Range Rover. As it pulled closer, he levered himself out of the chair and ambled over, waving to get Mike's attention.

"You alright, Tolly? How's your hip?"

Tolly waved away his concern. "We hired bicycles this morning; my hip's fine, it's the old legs that are suffering… takes a while to get accustomed."

"Sounds great." Mike was enthusiastic about anything outdoors. "Everyone have a good time?"

Tolly pulled a face and gestured towards Heather's tent. "It wasn't a roaring success," he whispered. "The only pub for miles was closed and, on the way back, Heather had a nasty accident."

"Oh? She alright?"

"I can hear you." Heather appeared at the opening to her tent and Mike turned round, smiling. He took a step backwards, recoiling when he saw her.

"Jesus, Heather! What have you done?"

She lowered her face. "A pigeon decided to play pinball with my head-"

"A pigeon?"

She nodded. "It flew over a hedge and hit me in the eye-"

"Ouch!"

"Even better, I fell off my bike into nettles."

"Bloody hell." Mike peered at her injuries. He had a look on his face as if he'd just discovered a packet of mouldy cheese in his fridge. Tolly waited for his reaction.

"Don't laugh." Heather looked defiantly between them. "It really hurts."

"I bet it does. It looks painful."

Tolly was grateful that Mike maintained a serious face.

"So much for a relaxing holiday," she grumbled, "now look at me."

"It's not *that* bad." Mike wasn't convincing anyone. He looked to Tolly for support.

"No, I've seen much worse," Tolly agreed. He *had* seen worse, but normally at Army boxing matches—but he didn't think he should add that bit.

"You don't need to humour me. I know I look like I've gone ten rounds with Tyson Fury," Heather whispered.

"You do not," Tolly replied.

"Not many people go ten rounds; two maybe," Mike quipped, and the two men chuckled. They stopped immediately on seeing Heather's glare and Mike cleared his throat.

"Anyway, I just thought I'd pop up to check on you all; see how you're getting on."

"Don't mind me," Heather pointed to her tent. "You two carry on. I'm going to get some more pills." She slouched off and climbed into her tent. Tolly pulled a face at Mike.

"Not a happy bunny," he stated quietly.

"No, that looked really sore."

Tolly caught Mike's eye then looked away quickly, feeling a chuckle rising in his throat. The last thing Heather needed was to hear the two of them making fun of her.

"So," Mike cleared his throat, "how is everything really?"

"Oh fine, fine." Tolly waved him towards the circle of chairs and sat down. "It has been a relaxing few days so far." He paused, then leant in. "It's been a bit boring really," he whispered. "Until the pigeon today, nothing has happened. We can't get to the Tower—the whole reason we came here—so I'm still in limbo."

"With Morris, you mean?"

Tolly nodded.

"Is there nowhere else you can scatter him?"

Tolly shook his head. "No, absolutely not. I promised him it would be at the Tower, overlooking the ocean." Tolly had made that commitment and he wouldn't be moved on it.

"You could do the detour and walk the long way round to the Tower?"

Again, Tolly shook his head.

"Not until we know what's happening up there. Suppose I scatter him then the Tower is made out of bounds." He tutted. "No, I just need to wait until we know what's going on." He clasped his hands in his lap and twiddled his thumbs. The quiet enveloped them for a few seconds then he sighed.

"The truth is that Eddie finds it a bit… morbid. She doesn't like having the urn on the mantelpiece." He smiled wryly. "But there's nothing I can do about it. Morris can't be at peace until he's at the Tower. It's all rather unsatisfactory isn't it, old bean?"

"I'm sure Eddie understands that you need to keep your promise," Mike added. The Tower held importance for lots of people and at the moment it wasn't satisfactory for any of them.

"Will you take her out?" Eddie whispered as Mike returned his empty mug to the kitchen area. They glanced over to where Heather sat, next to a smoking campfire, cradling her drink. "She's really down in the dumps. It might do her good to talk to someone her own age."

Mike shrugged; "I'm not sure how I can cheer her up. It's a bit awkward… I'm friends with her *and* Amir."

"Please Mike. I've no idea what's going through her head at the moment. She won't speak to me and I'm worried about her."

"Alright," he agreed reluctantly, "just for half an hour, then I must get home." He sauntered over to Heather and pasted a smile on his face. "Fancy going for a quick drink, while your mum cooks your dinner?"

Heather looked at him. "You not staying to eat?"

He shook his head; he was excited about seeing Phoebe again. As Heather looked at him, he had to steel himself from wincing as the visible sliver of her bloodshot eye moved. It could barely be seen below her puffed up lid.

"I don't want to *see* anyone," she said immediately.

"A walk then… you could wear a cap to cover your face?"

"Thanks Mike. Make a girl feel good, why don't you."

He backtracked, "just so it's not obvious… not because it looks awful."

"It's okay Mike, I know it's bad."

She did as he suggested and borrowed a baseball cap from her mum before they walked towards the coast path. The evening was glorious, the sun shining, and Mike found himself forgetting about the heavy workload that waited for him back in his office. Heather relaxed too. She seemed to forget about the shiner on her face until, on two occasions, she stumbled, her hand flying up to her face as the jolt made it hurt. They discussed her work, the camping—anything except Amir—and Mike was impressed by how far she'd come with her designs. She opened up to him, talking freely, and he felt a warm glow that she was able to confide in him.

"I could get one of my legal team to check any contracts, if you ever need help."

Heather glanced across and smiled. "That's kind of you, Mike, thank you."

As they reached the cliffs Mike pointed to a bench. On the edge of the gravel path, it had a perfect view across the bay. "Shall we take a pew?" They settled, side by side, and stared out across the blue expanse.

"Beautiful, isn't it?"

Heather nodded.

"So, ignoring the pigeon mishap today, has the week been okay otherwise?"

She tipped her head from side to side, considering the question. "It's been okay. It's made me realise I could do with friends of my own, though. Mum and Tolly are great, but I need to widen my circle; it's something when your mum has more fun than you."

"What about the woman who lives opposite? I thought you were going to meet up with her?"

Heather pondered. "Sophie? I was, wasn't I?" She sat, quiet with her thoughts as they stared into the distance. "But then I met Amir, and you lot. With my new business and opening the camp shop it was such a whirlwind. I hardly had enough time to spend with him, let alone anyone else." She pulled a sad face, "ouch, that hurts." She gingerly touched her face. "I thought he was all I needed," she added quietly.

"You haven't been here that long really," Mike nudged the conversation away from Amir. "You'll make friends soon," he glanced across. "Now your work is settling down maybe you could join a club or go out with Sophie."

Heather looked at him, a wistful expression on her face. "You're right, I'll ask her when I'm back. She's bound to know loads of people; she's very well connected." She gave a flicker of a smile and in that instant Mike sensed her loneliness; *he'd* been like that, until recently. All work and no play. This last couple of weeks he'd felt lighter and more positive. A thought dawned on him; it was because of Phoebe. Now he had something to look forward to. He nudged Heather with his elbow.

"You'll be alright."

She nodded. "You're sweet, Mike. Thank you." She leaned against him, and he expected her to move straight back. But she remained, their arms touching.

"You're a good confidante, Mike. I feel better whenever I offload to you." She put her head on his shoulder and relaxed; he felt the weight shift onto him. He stiffened; why wasn't she moving? It was good that she was comfortable with him, but this was a bit *too* close. He wanted to slide along the bench but didn't want to offend her; not when she was feeling vulnerable.

"This is nice," she whispered and he wondered how long he had to stay there before he could get up again.

Amir pulled his van into the car park and snatched up the handbrake. If he didn't do this now, he was going to chicken out and then they'd never talk to each other ever again—which would be ridiculous. He loved Heather.

"Amir! What are you doing here?" Tolly appeared, striding towards the van.

"I've come to see Heather. I need to talk to her."

"Righto, well she's gone for a walk with Mike. They headed towards the coast. Would you like a cup of tea first? Come and join us." Tolly pointed towards the camp and Eddie, poking her head out the tent at the sound of a visitor, waved energetically.

"Hi Eddie! No, I won't, thanks. I need to speak to Heather and if I don't do it now, I might lose my nerve."

"Good for you. Seize the day, grasp the nettle." Tolly drifted off, running out of metaphors, as Amir turned and walked towards the coast path.

"Wish me luck," he waved, taking long strides in his favourite walking boots. Today was a good day. He felt positive and in control of his destiny. Walking along the coastal path he paused to take in the view. He was momentarily distracted before the face of a smiling Heather popped into his head and he was spurred on. Rounding the corner, he saw the two of them sitting on a bench. They looked cosy, Heather's head on Mike's shoulder. Amir frowned. He slowed to watch, bobbing down by the hedge, hidden from view. This was unexpected. He waited, suddenly unsure of the firm plan he'd had before. He thought Heather still had feelings for him, but now he wasn't so sure. She lifted her head and gazed at Mike. They were sitting really close. Had Mike already moved in on his girlfriend? His heart squeezed as he realised that, technically, she wasn't his girlfriend anymore. Amir didn't want to interrupt them; he didn't want to make a fool of himself. Maybe he'd call round when she was back home. They could have a proper conversation, without an audience.

He took a step back. He was about to leave when Heather moved, her head looking towards Mike, their faces so close and then—Amir couldn't believe it—they were kissing. His stomach plummeted down to his hiking boots; he'd seen enough. If she'd forgotten him already, well he'd just leave her to it. She knew where to find him if she wanted to talk. He turned on his heel and stormed back to the campsite. He clenched and unclenched his jaw as he fought the anger, the humiliation. Did everyone know they were an item? Back at his van, he was fumbling with the keys when Tolly came over.

"Couldn't you find them?"

"Oh, I found them alright. They were very cosy on a bench up there."

Tolly frowned. "Did you speak to them?"

Amir shook his head. "No," he snorted. "I didn't want to interrupt them, they looked happy; just the two of them." He opened the door. "Sorry, Tolly, I really need to get going. See you soon, yeah?" He climbed in and waited for Tolly to move, before slamming the van into gear and zooming off down the track.

Heather leapt back and clamped her mouth shut. "I'm so sorry Mike, I shouldn't have done that."

Mike's mouth dropped open; he was stunned.

"I'm really sorry, I shouldn't have… can we just forget it?"

Mike visibly relaxed. "You caught me off guard. I didn't mean-"

"Mike, please stop! It shouldn't have happened. I got caught up in the moment." Heather put distance between them on the bench and for a moment they sat in silence. "I don't really think of you in that way," she added quietly, staring out to sea.

"No. Me neither-"

"Thank goodness," her laugh sounded shrill. "No offence but that just didn't feel right."

Mike turned to look at her. "No, it didn't."

"It didn't, did it?" She watched his face eagerly and when he shook his head, she laughed. "It didn't rock your world, did it?"

Mike paused, then shook his head. He looked apologetic.

"Not the same as when you kiss Phoebe?"

Colour started to creep up his face as he shook his head again.

"No, me neither. Honestly, Mike, can we just forget it?"

He nodded. "I'm sorry, Heather-"

"Don't be. It's helped. Given me clarity. I really should be sorting things out with Amir."

"Finally!" Mike threw his hands in the air, exasperated. "I wondered when you two would see sense."

Heather was thoughtful. "If it means kissing a few toads… oh sorry Mike."

"How rude!"

They both burst out laughing.

"I think I know what you mean." He took a playful swipe at her leg as she hopped up from the bench.

"Let's just forget that ever happened. You like Phoebe, and I need to go and see Amir." Heather was back in control; her earlier embarrassment now gone. "It reinforces what we already know, doesn't it?"

Mike nodded, "Yes, you're right. It does." He jumped up. "Phoebe! I forgot, I'm supposed to be picking them up."

As they made their way back Heather had a spring in her step that she'd not had for days. Reaching the camp, a smile was on her face; at last, it felt as if the universe was beginning to align for her. Hearing them approach, Tolly appeared from his tent.

"There you are! Did you see Amir?"

Heather shook her head, exchanging a glance with Mike. "Amir?"

Mike returned her look, his eyes clouding with worry.

"Yes, he was here about twenty minutes ago. He set off to find you, then came back and zoomed away."

Heather's aligning universe suddenly span out of control, making her stomach sink.

"He said he didn't want to disturb you as you looked," Tolly made quote marks, "'very cosy on a bench'."

Mike groaned and caught his lip between his teeth.

"What?" Tolly asked, "what happened?"

Heather shook her head, flustered. "We were just sitting on the bench together."

Mike nodded, confirming her words.

"I had my head on Mike's shoulder. Amir must have got the wrong end of the stick." She stood and pulled her phone from her pocket. "I'd better call him; we need to chat."

"And I *really* need to get going. I'm due at Phoebe's-" Mike glanced at his watch and gulped, "oh no, in ten minutes."

Chapter Twenty

Amir sighed as he placed the two mugs of tea on the shop's counter. Jack stopped stroking the arm of a fleece jacket and walked back towards him.

"Will you cheer up, Amir? You'll put the customers off with that face." The fleece was new in stock. Jack had popped in after college to help arrange the display and seemed very taken with it—Amir expected to be asked for a staff discount!

"What is wrong with you?" Jack nudged his arm as he reached the counter and Amir couldn't help but sigh again.

"This place. It's like a graveyard."

"And you're behaving like an undertaker, mooching around."

Amir glared at him, his dark eyes narrowing.

"This was your dream, remember. You're here, making it happen. I don't understand what your problem is."

"It's not as much fun as I thought it would be."

"What?" Jack turned to him and counted on his fingers. "Running your own business; no parents watching your every move; your own place upstairs and," he waggled his fingers at him, "– best of all, you get to play with all the stock. What's not to like?"

Amir's face lit up for an instant before it fell again. He took a deep breath and mirrored the action of counting on his fingers. "One, it's quite lonely; two, it's not that busy most of the time; three, I'm rattling around that huge flat upstairs and, four, sales aren't exactly rivalling Amazon, are they?"

Jack shrugged. "It'll pick up, don't worry." He shuffled his feet. "Amir, is it really about the shop, or something else? Cos ever since you went to see Heather you've seemed, well, dejected and angry, both at the same time." Jack watched for his reaction and when Amir didn't speak, he picked up his tea. The silence in the shop was broken by the sound of his slurping.

"I think it might be over with Heather."

Jack put his mug on the counter. "Why d'you think that?"

"She seems to have moved on."

Jack narrowed his eyes at him. "So, this *is* about Heather?"

Amir shrugged. "Partly—who could blame her? I was hardly around for her, was I? Working in here all the time."

"That's cos you're stubborn and won't let anyone help you."

"But I'm responsible for it; it's my shop-"

"I know boss, but plenty of us have offered to help. You don't need to be such a-" Jack stopped himself from going further. "Just take a break; let others help."

Amir tidied the boxes on the counter; one neatly stacked with Kendal Mint Cake, a larger box of assorted pocket torches and a tall, thin display of coloured rain ponchos. It was a distraction.

"It could give you time to meet Heather, do something nice, talk properly?"

The bell tinkled above the door, preventing Amir from responding. A young couple walked in, dressed for the outdoors. They were already halfway through a hike if their rosy cheeks were anything to go by. The woman strode towards them and placed an empty water bottle on the counter.

"Hi there," she smiled, displaying a neat row of white teeth. "Would you have anything like that? It's developed a crack and all my water's leaked out."

"We do indeed." Amir led them to the end of the room, shuffling around the tent display in the middle. Camping chairs and a table were arranged next to it, with cooking equipment, a camp bed and sleeping bag on the floor—highlighting what every busy customer needed for a trip away. Amir waved to a full-width shelf on the back wall.

"There are several different types there. Three-quarters of a litre, aluminium; that's the most popular. There's also a one litre flask or eight-hundred mill plastic bottles with isotherm holders."

The woman raised her eyebrows and took a step forward. "Thanks. Can I take a look?"

"Course," Amir nodded, "Give me a shout if you need me." As he went back behind the counter, Jack nudged his arm.

"See," he whispered, "you're a natural. It'll pick up."

Amir nodded, conscious that the customers were within earshot. He picked up his mug and took a sip instead. "How many boxes are there still in the back?"

Jack held up two fingers.

"Let's finish our tea, then we'll carry on. It'd be good to get some photos for Instagram, too."

The door opened again, and they both looked up as someone entered the shop. Whoever it was, was hidden behind an enormous bunch of beautifully wrapped, white lilies which appeared to float towards the counter. Jack took a step back before his face became engulfed. As the lilies were laid carefully on the counter, Heather appeared from behind, looking sheepish. Jack smiled then winced when he noticed her black eye and bruising.

"Jeez, Heather," he blurted. "What happened to you?"

"Jack!" Amir scowled.

"What?" Jack pointed to her face and they both watched, as Heather tenderly felt around her eye socket.

"A fight with a pigeon—he came off worse." She smiled then stopped, it clearly caused her pain.

"Seriously?" Jack leant closer, studying the bluish-purple tint.

"Yep. I was on a bike, and the pigeon flew out—straight into my face."

"Bloody hell."

"Yes, bloody hell." She turned slightly to smile at Amir. "Hi," she whispered. "These are for you."

"Oh." He searched for something to say, clearing his throat. "They're nice, er, thanks?" He stroked one of the petals, concentrating on the arrangement of spots on the inside, before looking back at her. "What are they for?"

"A peace offering. You didn't return my call."

"I was busy."

The air became still, as they studied each other. Amir didn't breathe, although his heart was racing. He tried to ignore Jack, who was looking from one to the other of them, as if watching a game of tennis. "I wasn't ready to talk to you," he whispered, truthfully.

"We need to, at some point."

"I'm not sure we've got much to talk about. It looked quite-" he glanced at Jack then back to Heather, "clear cut, from what I saw earlier."

Jack's eyebrows shot up, curious. Now Amir would have to explain what he'd seen—and feel the humiliation all over again. The sound of footsteps interrupted them, and the couple reappeared. Amir had forgotten they had customers in the shop as, tentatively, the woman held a bottle out, sensing she was disturbing something important.

"Er, could I get this one?"

"Sorry, of course." Jack stepped forward and nudged Amir away from the till. "Maybe you two…" he waved his hand for them to move away. "I'll help the customer." He picked up the flowers. "These'll need water," he added, pressing them into Amir's chest, scrunching the green tissue paper as he did so. Amir hesitated. He should be dealing with the customer but rather than make a scene, he took the lilies.

"I'll leave you with Jack," he said to the woman then put a hand on Heather's back and guided her to the other side of the shop.

"Aluminium, good choice!" Jack's voice sounded loud and unnatural as Amir followed Heather. They moved round the camping display and leaned against the wall. Amir peered over the flowers. "What do you want, Heather? This isn't really a good time." He was weary and her appearance in his workplace had stirred up conflicting emotions. Heather pointed to the tent.

"Can we go in there?"

"What for?"

"I dunno. It just looks more private than standing out here."

Amir shrugged. "It's not. But if it makes you happy." He placed the flowers on the floor, then crawled into the tent following Heather. They sat cross legged, opposite each other. Amir's knees creaked at being forced into this unnatural position; for the sake of his joints, he hoped the chat would be quick.

"I came to apologise. To explain about what you may think you saw."

"What I actually *saw*," Amir hissed, "was my girlfriend kissing another man."

She put her finger to her lips. "Shush." She thumbed towards Jack and the customers, as outside the till pinged open, and Jack's voice floated across the shop.

"That's no problem," he said, loudly. "I'll just go and fill it up for you."

The till slammed and Amir saw Jack's shadow move around the tent.

"I'm just going to fill this bottle with tap water," he said pointedly, nudging the tent as he inched past and went through to the kitchen beyond. They waited. The tap ran next door then Jack's outline reappeared, squeezing round them again and disappearing back to the counter. They heard footsteps, the bell tinkled then the door closed.

"They've gone. You can carry on," Jack shouted. "I'm not listening."

For a moment neither of them spoke.

"So! Why *were* you…" Amir lowered his voice, "kissing Mike? I'd love to know." He folded his arms.

Heather sighed. "Did you not listen to the message?"

"*Of course* I did."

"Well, I explained, didn't I?"

"Not really. I don't understand how you can be friends with someone then suddenly be snogging."

"We weren't snogging-" she hissed, frowning for him to keep his voice down.

"It *looked* like snogging from where I was."

"Shush."

"Don't tell me to shush," Amir thumbed to where he imagined Jack to be standing. "He probably knows everything anyway; I imagine I'm the last to know about what's going on."

Heather tutted, her face flushing. "Don't be childish."

"Childish!"

Heather held her hands up. They both stopped and glared at each other, breathing heavily. Heather exhaled, moving her hands with her breath to encourage them both to remain calm.

"I'm sorry, Amir. I really am. I shouldn't have kissed him; I was at a very low ebb." She held a hand up as he started to protest. "Please, just let me say this-"

"But it looked like you were ecstatic at being kissed."

"Not being kissed no, but it was *good* that I kissed him."

Amir's mouth dropped open. He couldn't believe she was admitting it.

"Yes, it was good," she emphasised "*because* I felt nothing from it."

"Bully for you," he scowled. "Anyone else you'd like to try out-"

"It made me realise that it's *you* I love."

Amir blinked. His knees were shouting at him, making it difficult to think straight. He adjusted his position and pulled them towards him instead. That was better.

"Funny way of showing it," he said grumpily. "Moving out and leaving me."

"I was trying to force you into action. We couldn't go on as we were. You were working all the time, not letting anyone else help."

"It's my shop-"

"Yes, we know it's your shop. But you pushed me away, working all the time. *And* you made me feel guilty for any success I had."

"Hold on. Are you saying this is my fault?"

She seemed to have forgotten about her apology and he didn't like the way she was laying it all at his door. "I didn't force you into Mike's arms."

Heather slumped over; her knees were obviously more flexible than his ever would be.

"I'm not saying that. I'm trying to explain why I left in the first place."

"Because you didn't have my undivided attention? I'm sorry I was busy, but you can't turn this on me. I was working all hours to get this place off the ground. If it was a true relationship, we'd be in it together—not running off to someone else, snogging, as soon as the going got tough."

"I tried to help-"

"When you weren't drawing," he said with a sneer.

"I was also trying to get *my* business off the ground, remember?"

"And haven't you just… little Miss Successful?" As soon as he'd said it, he wanted to rewind; pull the words from the air and shove them back in his mouth.

"You're jealous." She spoke slowly, studying him with a new understanding. "Is that what this is about? Your pride is hurting."

Amir didn't speak. Maybe he was. Financially, she was doing much better than him. Maybe he had pushed her away, and others too. Hadn't Jack said the same thing just a few minutes ago?

"I could have helped you, given you a break. But there are only so many times you can offer and be told 'no'." She took his hand in hers and stroked it with her thumb. "I felt ignored, surplus to requirements."

"So, you found someone who *did* require you?"

Heather's eyes stared at him, emotionless; the swollen, purple skin around one looked sore and he itched to caress it, to make it all better. Why had he said that? He knew why… because of Mike. Despite her declaration of love for him, she'd still kissed Mike. He couldn't get past that fact. Oh, what a mess!

Heather slumped forwards. "You know, this isn't getting us very far. I'm going to go now. Mike was a huge mistake. We both recognised it immediately. I love *you*; I want *us* to be together. But we," she waved her hand backwards and forwards between them, "can't be, until you treat us as a team. I can help you in the shop, we *all* want to help, but you're so stubborn and it's not *just* about you." She pushed herself onto all fours and leant across to kiss his cheek. "Call me when you're ready to talk properly." She crawled out the tent. He heard her say 'bye' to Jack then the bell tinkled. The air felt different. She'd gone. He stretched his legs out, then turned onto all fours and crept out the tent. Jack was standing outside, his arms folded, his forehead furrowed.

"You're a right prat sometimes." He put out a hand to pull Amir off the floor. "Seriously, boss? Heather and Mike?" He tutted. "That would never work in a million years; and the sooner you realise that…" shaking his head, Jack walked to the front of the shop and continued to unpack the new stock.

Chapter Twenty-One

Phoebe buttered the toast and picked up the pan. Bugger! She scraped the beans off the bottom; they'd have to do.

"Celeste. Come and get your beans."

Her daughter bounded into the kitchen and skidded to a halt on the tiled floor. Her lower half was ready for the ballet concert—dainty pink tights and a blush-coloured tutu—the top half less so, in a multi-coloured Ariana Grande hoodie.

"Ugh, beans." With her bottom lip sticking out, she begrudgingly took the offered plate and sat at the table.

"I know it's not great, sweetheart, but eat what you can. Mike's coming to give us a lift and perhaps, on the way home, we can stop at the chip shop."

Her daughter's face instantly brightened. "Mike's coming? Yay." She forked in a mouthful of beans, chewed, and swallowed. In her new-found excitement about Mike and possible chips, she didn't even seem to register that she was eating them.

Phoebe looked anxiously out the front window, waiting for the Range Rover to pull up. Celeste sat on the bottom step in the hall, tying up her trainers. A bag, next to her, contained her beloved pink ballet pumps and top; with a t-shirt, leggings and socks to change into after. Phoebe glanced at her watch. It had just gone quarter to, and she could feel her heart rate increasing. Where was he? She took in a deep breath and tried to remain calm. He'd be here. He said he would be. A noise in the back of her mind started to rumble. She recognised it; the voice of anxiety from over the years and it had reappeared a few times since yesterday. But Mike wasn't anything like Eric, she reminded herself; he was more mature for one thing, and he was responsible and caring. So where is he?

Celeste skipped into the living room.

"I've got my trainers on, mama. Ready to go?" She joined her mum at the window and they both looked out. "Where's Mike?"

"He'll be here soon, darling. Don't you worry."

Celeste sagged to the floor. She stretched out and stared at the ceiling. "This is going to be so great," she said, moving her legs and arms as if making a snow angel.

"Don't do that, Celeste, not with your trainers on."

Celeste stopped. She lay still and eyed her mum, silence descended on the room. With a loud intake of breath, Celeste turned her ear to the ground.

"I'll see if I can hear him."

Phoebe looked at her watch. Nearly five to seven. She rubbed her chin. How much longer could she wait? She looked through the window, still no sign of him. They were going to be late. She glanced at Celeste, who grinned back, oblivious to the thoughts running riot in Phoebe's head. Celeste was so excited about this evening, if she missed the concert… well, it was unthinkable. A ball of anger started to spread from Phoebe's tummy. Maybe she was wrong about him. Maybe now he'd reeled her in his true personality would come out; she was already suspended from work because of the Wanderers. The worry was replaced by anger; anger directed at Mike for causing this turmoil, these feelings of insecurity and uncertainty. She took out her phone and dialled the taxi company.

"Yes, taxi as soon as possible please. Uh huh…" she listened. "Need to be at St Luke's church by 7.15 please. We're Bede Street." She waved a hand at Celeste to get up. She grabbed her coat and handbag and opened the front door. "Okay, we'll walk along the street towards the Newsagents. Yes. Okay, thanks." She hung up and ushered Celeste out, locking the door behind them. "Right, we need to get a wriggle on. The taxi will pick us up at the end of the road. Let's go."

They moved briskly, alternating between speed walking, and running. Celeste didn't complain. She knew when her mum was on a mission and Phoebe's mouth was set firm. She was in no mood for discussion. The taxi was at the corner when they got there. She opened the door, pushed Celeste in, then followed her onto the back seat.

"Thank you for this, I'm sorry about the rush." She spoke to the driver between snatches of breath.

"No problem, love." He turned the radio up and put his foot down, the car pulled smoothly away. Phoebe sank into the seat and closed her eyes. That was the very last time she trusted a man and, lost in thought, she closed her eyes only to reopen them minutes later when they pulled up outside the church.

"Six pounds please, love." The man pulled the handbrake on and turned round.

"You go in," she whispered to Celeste, "I'll be right behind you." Celeste looked at her, suddenly less sure of herself. "Go," Phoebe urged, "you'll be late. I'll be right behind you."

Celeste opened the door. "You will come, won't you?"

"Darling, of course I'm coming. I just need to pay the man."

Celeste hopped out and ran along the path towards the church. Phoebe opened her bag and pulled out her card. The driver, spotting her method of payment, held up the machine and she tapped it. She waited for the clearance. Instead, she heard a beep.

"Sorry love. It's not gone through. Try again?"

She tapped again and held her breath. There should be enough in her account to cover six quid. It was nearly pay day, and she was still in credit—just. The machine beeped again. Obviously not. Sweat prickled the back of her neck, as she ran through her options. Celeste would be wondering where she was. She opened her bag. Hidden under the Sexy Scarlet lipstick was her emergency ten-pound note. She handed it over.

"Sorry love," the driver turned but his seatbelt locked. With his head forward, he manipulated his mouth as far left as he could, talking over his shoulder. "I've not got change for that."

"But it's all I have," Phoebe replied, running her hand around her bag in the hope that some pound coins would be hiding. They weren't. "Don't you have a kitty or something?"

"Normally I would, love, I'd get change from the depot, but I haven't been in yet." His mouth returned to normal. "I picked you up on my way… as a favour to the gaffer, like."

Now she felt bad for disrupting their system. "Oh, I see, and thanks; we'd not have made it otherwise." She held out the tenner. "Here. Keep the change… for your trouble."

"No trouble, love."

She collected her coat and Celeste's bag and hopped out. "Thanks," she managed, before slamming the door. She breathed in. She felt the familiar vibrating of her phone. Mike.

"Yes?"

"Phoebe. Where are you?"

"At the church."

"But I said I'd-"

"You were late. I didn't know what to do, so I called a cab."

"I got caught up with something. I'm outside yours now. I'll come straight over."

"Mike, I need to go." She nodded towards Celeste who was hopping from foot to foot in the doorway, beckoning her in.

"Come on mama," she shouted.

"Phoebe, I'm sorry. I'll come-"

"Mike, I really need to go. I'm late." She hung up and marched forwards. "Come on then," she spoke to Celeste, "what are you waiting for?" She smiled at her excited daughter, but the smile didn't quite reach her eyes.

"Did you like it? Were you watching me?"

The performance, by the small troop of nine-year-olds, had been surprisingly good and Phoebe had found herself caught up in the music and their movements. At one point the main door had rattled and, thinking it was Mike she'd turned, ready to give him a stony stare. Disappointment, however, had flooded in; it was just the wind catching the door and she berated herself for even being bothered. She wasn't ready to forgive him yet. Her thoughts turned to Eric. How different could life have been if he'd been interested in sharing these moments with his daughter? Was Celeste missing out by not having a father figure in her life?

"Mum, are you okay?"

Phoebe turned back to her daughter who'd stopped hopping about with the other tutu-clad dancers. She nudged closer against Phoebe's legs.

"I'm fine, sweetheart. You were a-maz-ing! How you remembered all those moves I'll never know!" She took her daughter's hand and, squeezing it, smiled at the innocent face staring back. Phoebe's only job in this world was to look after her and to make sure Celeste knew she'd always be there for her. As soon as other people got involved, there was trouble. She pictured Thomas Johnson's face, and Evelyn marching her out of the building. She'd enjoyed meeting the Wanderers, but she was now on the brink of losing her job because she'd let them in. She kissed Celeste's cheek. No, they were better off alone—just the two of them—and Agnes, of course.

Unfortunately, Celeste hadn't got that memo. When she spotted Mike leaning patiently against his car outside, she broke into a run. He smiled when he saw her and bent down to listen as she described the whole performance in minute detail.

"It sounded like quite a show," he said, giving her a round of applause. "I'm really sorry I missed it."

"It's okay." Celeste was more forgiving than Phoebe. "There'll be another at Christmas anyway." She hopped down the path on one leg.

"I am really sorry, Phoebe. I got caught up and didn't realise the time. I was at yours for seven so we could have made it."

"Maybe."

"Can I give you a lift home? It's the least I can do."

She shrugged. She didn't want to talk to him, but they did need to get home and she had no cash and a dodgy bank card to boot. The doors to the car unlocked with a soft thump and Celeste ran back to join them. Phoebe strapped her in the backseat then joined Mike. As the car purred down the road Phoebe settled against the leather seats, but she couldn't allow herself to relax. She glanced in the back. Celeste's eyes had already closed, tired out from an exciting evening. She'd obviously forgotten about the promise of chips.

"Was she late for the performance?" Mike asked, softly.

"No, we got there in time. A cab was passing on his way, so he stopped for us."

"That was lucky."

"Yes, it was." She didn't have the energy to explain about the ten pounds and how, as a result, she'd have to change her routine to go via the ATM in the morning. He wouldn't understand the stress of having to watch every penny. They drove the rest of the way in silence and pulled up outside her home. Mike cut the engine and glanced into the back. Celeste was fast asleep.

"Do you want me to carry her in?"

"It's fine, I can do it."

Mike put his hand on her arm. "I know I messed up, Phoebe. I'm sorry." He removed his hand. "Let me carry her indoors for you. It's the least I can do."

Phoebe relented. "She can go straight to bed; she's going to be tired tomorrow." She climbed out the car and waited for him to pick up her daughter. She unlocked the front door. Mike cradled Celeste in his arms and climbed the stairs; Phoebe followed. Carefully, he laid her down in her single bed then hovered by the door while she removed Celeste's trainers and pulled the cover over her. Back downstairs Mike stood by the front door.

"I'll leave you to it, it's getting late."

She nodded and thumbed towards the kitchen. "I need to tidy up. It's a tip through there."

"Can I call you, maybe do something another evening?"

Phoebe leant against the wall and looked at her shoes. They weren't her favourite polka dot ones, but these were almost as good—lime green with blue bows on the front to go with her navy three-quarter length trousers.

"I don't think I can do this, Mike."

"Just because I was late?" He frowned. "I *was* coming for you."

"I didn't know that. I couldn't risk it." She took a deep breath. "Celeste has to be my priority."

Mike took a step towards her. "I was *ten* minutes late."

"It's not just that." She paused and could feel Mike holding his breath. "I've been suspended from work."

"What?" Incredulous he reached out to her, but she held her hands up.

"Don't, Mike. It's been lovely going out with you. You're really nice, but I can't do this."

"Do what?"

"Everything just needs to go back to how it was. I can't afford to lose my job; I can't afford to get distracted."

He made to speak but she cut him off.

"I *am* getting distracted; I was looking into Gundry's Tower, to try to please you; and I altered my usual plans because you'd offered to take us tonight."

He reached out to her, but she shook her head.

"Don't please, Mike. Don't make it any harder than this already is. You're lovely," she looked into his eyes, and registered the surprise in them. "I really thought we could have made a go of it, but I can't let my guard down. I'm not going through that again." Tears appeared in her eyes, and she sniffed, trying to regain her control.

"Phoebe," he said quietly, "this is crazy. I won't hurt you, and I'm sure your work is a misunderstanding-"

"A misunderstanding that's got me sent home and waiting for a disciplinary hearing."

Confused, Mike frowned at her. "But why, what's the reason for that?"

"Not following management instruction," she whispered, the thought of it making her eyes water again.

"But that's wrong, surely. You should be at liberty to check for the public record." He paused, his frown deepening. "It really sounds as if there's something not right there. You can't blame the Wanderers for that. I wonder if I-"

"That's what I'm saying—I don't need your help to bail me out. I was fine on my own before and I'll be fine again."

"But Phoebe-"

"Please Mike, just go. I'm tired." She walked to the front door and held it open for him. He followed then paused, holding her gaze. He *was* lovely and it was taking all her willpower not to pull him towards her and kiss him. He was so in control of his life whereas she was a jabbering wreck; her life spiralling out of control.

"Please understand; I have to consider Celeste."

"But, this makes no-"

She needed to think, to put some distance between them. "Mike. I really need to tidy up."

"Okay. Can I call you in the week?"

She pushed her hair back from her face, tucking one curl behind her ear. She bit her lip, refusing to make eye contact. He sighed, then leant forwards and kissed her cheek.

"Bye, Phoebe."

He left, walked down the path and climbed in his car. She heard the car start up, then watched as the tail lights disappeared down the street. As she pushed the door shut, her tears started to fall, and not for the first time she wondered if she was doing the right thing.

Chapter Twenty-Two

Phoebe woke with a snort and sat upright in bed. Her eyes flew to the clock on the bedside table, seven thirty, they needed to get moving. It wasn't until she was out of bed and had shoved her feet into her leopard-print slippers that she remembered. There was no rush, as other than getting Celeste to school, she had nowhere to be. This was the third morning that she'd done this. Now fully awake, she continued down to the kitchen and put the kettle on. She started to pull the ingredients for pancakes out of the cupboard. Focusing on the flour, eggs and milk meant that her head didn't have space for thoughts about work. An official letter had arrived from the Council yesterday, and she'd taken it round to open at Agnes's. They'd read it together, several times, until its content had sunk in. She was to go to the office next Tuesday for an official disciplinary meeting. The letter had laid out the charges being levelled against her. *Insubordination* and *failing to follow management instructions* were the top two and, under Agnes's supervision she'd made a list of things to say; Agnes had offered to practice her responses with her over the weekend. Phoebe's palms grew sweaty just thinking about it, but with Agnes's coaching she might be alright. She had the opportunity to take someone with her, but who? She sighed. She wasn't in a union, most of her friends were at work, and she didn't want to drag them into her mire. The main problem was that the only person she kept coming back to was Mike, but she seemed to have burnt those bridges too. He'd not contacted her since she'd practically thrown him out on Tuesday. She reached for the hand whisk and started to beat the batter, hard. She channeled her pent-up frustration against the eggs, and found it was surprisingly therapeutic. Footsteps on the stairs announced the arrival of a dozy Celeste. She stumbled into the kitchen, rubbing sleep from her eyes.

"What are you doing, mama?" She yawned and pulled a chair over to stand on, positioning it next to her mum.

"I," Phoebe plastered on a smile, "am making you pancakes."

Celeste immediately brightened. "Pancakes? Yippee, yippee…with chocolate and banana?"

Phoebe nodded and pointed to the fruit bowl before dragging out a frying pan. "You cut up the bananas and I'll get cracking."

They worked together, the radio on quietly in the background and soon they were sat down, working through a pile of pancakes. This was nice. She needed to savour these moments as, by next week, she hoped they'd be running around again, getting out the door to school and back to work.

After dropping Celeste off at school, Phoebe wandered into the High Street. It wasn't the quickest route home, but she had time to spare; plus, she wanted to buy paint for her shed. She'd cleaned the outside already, under the watchful eye of her neighbour, and they'd spent a companionable hour discussing the merits of painting it a nice bright colour versus a sensible brown or green to blend in with the garden. She paused to look in the window of a clothes shop then carried on. She had enough clothes and didn't dare put anything else on her credit card. A hot flush ran up her back; with all the drama on Monday she'd not got around to phoning the bank like she'd intended. She opened her bag, the bill was still lodged in the bottom; that was the last thing she needed, to be chased by bailiffs as well.

"Phoebe!"

She turned to see Rita waving and, while she waited for her to catch up, she shoved the envelope back inside.

"Hi Phoebe, I've been meaning to give you a bell, see if you found out anything about Gundry's." She paused to catch her breath and as the church clock struck nine thirty, a frown flickered across her face. "Aren't you working today?"

"Um, not working no."

"Oh nice. Got some time off."

"You could say that."

Rita's eyebrows twitched as Phoebe took a deep breath.

"Have you got time for a cuppa?"

When Rita nodded, Phoebe steered her into the art gallery and up the stairs to the artisan café. "You get us some seats," she pointed to a corner table, "I'll get us a large pot of tea for two; I've got a feeling we're going to need it."

"But that's outrageous. He can't do that." Rita's cheeks flushed pink.

"Well," Phoebe put a hand on her arm to calm her down, worried about the older woman's blood pressure. "He might not get away with it in the long term but for now, he can. And he has."

"Have you got a union rep involved? What do they think?"

Phoebe sighed. "I'm not in a union." She mashed the teabags and topped up their half-drunk cups. "I've made a list of things I've got to say, and hopefully they'll realise it's the Council's mistake."

"What is Thomas playing at?" Rita slurped her tea, her eyes on Phoebe. "Something doesn't add up, does it?"

Phoebe shook her head. "That's what Mike said," she whispered. "I don't understand why the information isn't on the website. It's standard procedure to document the surveys and provide an outline of the findings. The appeal should also be there, with reasons why it was declined. There's nothing." She sighed, these thoughts had been running round her head for days now and it was mentally draining. "And Thomas said the paperwork would be in Archives, but I found the file on his desk. If only I'd been able to read it before-"

"In fairness," Rita interrupted, "he might have thought it had been sorted."

"-he might. But why be so defensive about it. If it was a legitimate error, he should be thanking me for highlighting it. Why did he warn me off, remind me about job cuts? Why suspend me?"

Rita patted Phoebe's hand and shook her head. "I really don't get it," she stared at the tabletop where some granules of sugar had fallen. She pushed them around with her fingertip, clearly deep in thought.

"I've been trying to find out about the surveys too." Rita formed the granules into a circle. "*I* didn't do them, and I've asked the others, who usually provide cover, but none of them know anything. There is a limited number of us, unless Thomas has gone elsewhere." She looked at Phoebe and shrugged. "It's a possibility but unlikely." The two women sat musing. Rita finished her tea and put her cup down. "We really need to find out about the surveys."

"There was something from the Aurelius company-"

Rita shrugged, "not one I'm familiar with."

"I wish I'd been able to find out more," said Phoebe, raising her hands in frustration, "but look where it's got me."

"We just need to try a little harder." Rita swept the granules onto her palm and tipped them into her empty cup. "Come on, I've had an idea."

As they walked down the stairs into the art gallery, the sound of hammering made Phoebe look over. A woman stepped back to survey a large, landscape picture. She adjusted the levels then smiled, admiring her handiwork. She glanced their way.

"Hey, Phoebe! Nice to see you. And Rita, right?"

Tolly's daughter in law was recognisable by her messy hair bun but instead of walking boots and trousers, today she wore paint splattered leggings and a long, oversized jumper.

"Excuse my attire."

Phoebe stopped staring.

"I've been busy in my studio. I'm just getting the last canvas hung before my exhibition. It starts on Saturday."

"It's looking great," Phoebe smiled. "I didn't realise this was your work. I've noticed the paintings going up each day when I've walked Celeste to school."

Diana radiated excitement. "I'm really excited about it—you'll have to come," she nodded eagerly, "both of you." She dashed off to the counter and returned with two postcard sized invitations. "One for each of you. These scenes are a bit different from my recent work," she waved around the light room. "I used to paint a lot of landscapes but recently I've been concentrating on more contemporary, large-scale works," she leant in. "To be honest it's what the customers pay for," she smiled wryly, "but these give me so much pleasure that I'm going to compromise and seek some enjoyment too… a few hours a week, at least."

"Very sensible," Rita chipped in. "I do the same. Some consultancy to pay the bills, coupled with teaching at the university, which I love. It's all about a good balance."

"Exactly! So, what are you two ladies up to?" Diana looked between them.

"Oh, we just bumped into each other actually, having a quick catch up about some work." Rita smiled broadly, not skipping a beat and Phoebe could've kissed her for not spilling the beans about her current work dilemma.

"We were just on our way out but noticed these fantastic pictures."

"Have a browse if you want, although if you do come on Saturday there'll also be some warm fizz; I'm hoping it might improve the paintings for everyone." Diana laughed, self-deprecating, and Phoebe warmed to her even more; she wore her amazing talents very lightly.

"You are incredible, Diana," she said in awe, taking in the recently hung landscape. "That's a beauty."

"Ah, that's an early one of mine. Tolly found it in his attic last week," she whispered.

"You've captured so much detail; it must have taken ages."

Rita peered at it, leaning in closer. Diana frowned, watching her face as she scrutinized the brush strokes.

"I did it from start to finish in one day," Diana added. "James looked after Jack; he was only a baby. There's something about having a limited time frame so I just got on with it; I was very focused."

"Is it from a photo?" Rita's eyes remained on the painting.

"No." Diana pointed to the brickwork on the edge of the canvas. "It's Gundry's Tower; where we were last week."

"Yes, I recognise it." Rita whispered. Phoebe hadn't noticed the tower on the edge of the canvas.

"But you've added the flowers from a book or photo?"

"No." Diana frowned. "It was exactly like that."

"What, these flowers were at Gundry's Tower?" Rita's eyes flicked between Diana and the painting. "They were this colour, and this small? With these multiple petals?"

Diana nodded. "I thought they were beautiful. I sketched them exactly as they were."

Rita moved a step closer, inspecting the detail. "What time of year was it; can you remember?"

Intrigued by the questioning, Diana moved to stand beside Rita. "I can, actually. Jack was little. It had been really warm, April, possibly May."

"How long ago?"

"Um," Diana cast around. "Jack's eighteen, so seventeen years ago."

Rita sighed, her mouth moving from side to side.

"Rita, what's going on?" Phoebe nudged her friend's arm.

"I think these flowers are a particular type of orchid and, if they are, they're extremely rare." She looked at them both, her eyes gleaming. "I've never seen them outside protected sites in southern Europe." She sucked air in through her teeth. "But seventeen years ago?"

"No, they were still there recently… well, a couple of years ago," Diana nodded at Rita, the excitement clearly contagious. "We walked there." Diana ran her hand over her bun, causing more strands to escape. "Me, James, and Jack. In fact, I did another painting, similar to this one," she rubbed her chin, thinking. "It might be in the back; I could look for you?"

Rita shook her head, "no, don't worry." She stared at Phoebe. "We *really* need to find out about the surveys, come on." She turned and left the gallery.

Phoebe flashed a smile as they watched her departure.

"I think I need to go," she whispered. "We'll explain later, but thanks… really helpful."

"No problem. Let me know if I can do anything," Diana shouted as Phoebe ran out the gallery. Rita was a woman on a mission and Phoebe wanted to be with her.

Chapter Twenty-Three

Phoebe walked into her kitchen and paused, watching as Agnes sliced the block of cheese on the chopping board. She was cutting thin layers ready to toast under the grill and Phoebe worried that at any minute she'd slice through one of her fingers. Cheese on toast was one of Agnes's go-to favourites; she always said that she'd never been a fancy cook, nothing experimental, but *this* was her signature dish. Phoebe took a deep breath, savouring the smell of the cheese as it started to bubble under the heat.

"How is it going in there?" Agnes nodded through the doorway to where Rita was speaking into the phone. Phoebe shrugged.

"She's only just got through to someone."

Agnes pulled out the grill pan and seeing that the cheese was now melted, a little crispy on top just how she liked it, she sliced it into quarters and took it through to Phoebe's dining table.

"Here you are, tuck in." She placed it on the table as Rita hung up and looked at them, her face grim.

"Roddy's in a meeting. He should be available later to call me back."

Phoebe sighed; they'd just have to wait a bit longer.

"They asked if I wanted to speak to his deputy, Thomas Jo-"

"I hope you said 'no, you bloody didn't want to speak to that prick!'"

"Phoebe!" Agnes looked at her, eyebrows knitting together.

"Sorry."

"Of course I did," Rita said, picking up a piece of toast, "not quite in those words, obviously." She chomped down on the food and moaned in approval. "This is just what I needed. Thank you, Agnes."

"You're welcome, love." Agnes nibbled daintily around one quarter. "So, we've just got to wait then; be patient?"

"Yep. Looks like it." Rita reached for another slice. "I'll get off in a minute, leave you to it. I'll try again this afternoon and if I get any response, I'll let you know."

Phoebe drove along the narrow country lane, following the sign to the Queen's Hill care home. She'd been on her way to drop the car at the garage but had felt compelled to take the detour. She wasn't sure why, other than to see if there had been any further changes; had the diggers moved, had the work been postponed? As she slowly rounded the bend she stopped on a verge, the care home now in view towards the south. Unfortunately, the fencing and the heavy-duty equipment were also in sight next door; a gate was propped open into a neighbouring field and her heart hardened at the sight before her. The countryside was already being torn up, deep wide track marks from the diggers had cut through the grass, and it would only get worse if the developers got their way. Anger rose in her; how dare they destroy people's memories of this place, not to mention their ongoing enjoyment of it. The anger flared quickly then subsided into a trough of despair. What could she do about it; if Rita couldn't get anyone to take it seriously what hope did she have? The authorities were a faceless, impenetrable wall; how could normal people breach it? Or *could* they? She had an idea and reached for her phone. The engine idled as she scrolled through names on her phone; she didn't dare turn it off in case it didn't start again. She hit the connect button and waited as the tone changed to ringing.

"Good afternoon, Penny Duvall speaking."

"Penny! It's me, Phoebe-"

"Hi there," she sounded overly enthusiastic, and Phoebe wondered if there was someone in the office with her.

"Are you able to talk?"

"Yes, uh-huh. I think that's okay; could you give me a few more details and I'll look into it."

There was *definitely* someone in the office with her.

"Okay, I get it. I'll keep talking but if you need to hang up just do it; I'll call you back later. Sooo… I know I shouldn't be contacting you, but I really need your help."

"Uh-huh, okay."

This was very weird, to keep talking without any interaction from Penny, but Phoebe had to keep going.

"Rita and I have seen a picture that shows there were extremely rare flowers up at Gundry's Tower. We've been trying to find out if the surveys have been done correctly, but," she huffed, "as you know, that's not gone down very well. I don't know why but Thomas has blocked me at every opportunity. But time's running out and we can't get hold of Roddy, so I want to call Jason Turner."

"The Chief Exec?" Penny coughed then added, "yes, that's correct. Jason Turner is the Chief Executive."

"I know I'm asking a lot but is there any way you can find his number and call me back?"

"No problem. Happy to help. Thank you." She hung up. Phoebe stared at her phone. What did that mean? From her vantage point she saw a man walk across the field. Wearing boots, jeans and a fluorescent tabard he climbed into one of the trucks and revved its engine. He swung it in a big circle and without slowing down turned out of the field and onto the country road. Thick diesel puffed up behind the monster truck, the tracks flicking up clods of earth. Phoebe had an image of what the area would become over the next few weeks if she wasn't able to stop the development.

"Come on, Pen," she whispered, shaking her phone. As if in response it lit up. 'Penny Duvall' came up on the screen and she answered it straight away. "Hi, Pen."

"So, I've got his office number, best I could do I'm afraid. I'd better not hang around," she rattled off the landline number. "But Phoeb, it won't help you as he's on leave until Monday anyway."

"Monday will be too late," Phoebe whispered, a sob threatening to overtake her as waves of desperation washed over her. She felt so useless.

"Sorry Phoeb." The older woman sounded desolate, bringing Phoebe back to her senses; it wasn't Penny's fault.

"Thanks for trying anyway; we'll just have to keep our fingers crossed that Rita can get hold of Roddy before the weekend's over." She hung up and stared out the windscreen, shaking her head in frustration. She crossed her fingers, hopefully Roddy would call Rita back, then she could explain. Phoebe paused, leaning on the steering wheel. What if he didn't? She was always waiting for someone else to do something; her life in the hands of others, while she kept quiet and didn't rock the boat. Well, she gripped the wheel, she wasn't going to wait anymore. The land shouldn't be under threat because one person was on holiday, and another was in a meeting. *Someone* should be around with the authority to investigate this; and that needed to be *before* Monday when the diggers rolled in. She watched as two men walked over to a truck in the field. They lifted the bonnet, looking at something underneath. They'd not even noticed she was there. *No one* ever noticed she was there. Well, she had tried via the official routes with no effect. Now they needed to draw attention to what was unfolding. Phoebe didn't know where this sudden assertiveness was coming from, but she liked it. Enough was enough; no more sitting quietly, letting others ride roughshod; she was going to cause a storm.

Chapter Twenty-four

Phoebe sat on a red customer sofa at the local garage, waiting for news about her car. She needed to make a call and had been rehearsing this conversation on her drive back from the Tower. *Come on Phoeb*, she gave herself a pep talk before hitting the button from her contacts list. *You got this.* The phone rang a couple of times before being picked up.

"Phoebe?"

Her insides melted at the sound of Mike's voice.

"Hi, how are you? And Celeste?" He was still concerned about them, even after she'd been mean to him the other day. "I'm so pleased you've called; I didn't know whether to ring but thought I'd better give you some space."

"Mike," she whispered, clutching the phone to her ear. "I'm fine thank you." She smiled into the phone. "I'm better than fine actually-"

"Oh? What's happened, is it your work?"

"Sort of… I've been doing a lot of thinking. I am really sorry; I shouldn't have taken out my issues on you and blamed you for my trouble at work, you know, the whole suspension thing."

"Phoebe, I didn't mean-"

"No, I know you didn't. You've only ever tried to help me. I should have done things differently at work."

"I'm sorry-"

"Mike, it's okay. We're good, honestly. Listen, I've got an idea and I could really do with some help."

"Intriguing," he said quietly, his voice low over the phone. "I'll always help if I can. I've really missed you these last few days."

"Me too," she whispered, as butterflies flitted around her stomach. "One thing you said, about speaking up, really sank in." She paused. "Rita and I have been trying to find out about the surveys at Gundry's Tower."

"I thought you weren't allowed to contact anyone at the Council."

"I decided we didn't have time to play by the rules-"

"Phoebe Ellis, you maverick!"

That made her smile, and she leaned closer to the phone; she wished he was here in person rather than at the end of an echoing line.

"We can't find out any information, what surveys have been done or how many-"

"How many should there be?"

"Two. There should always be *at least* two, at different times of the year to make sure any growth is captured." She paused. "To make things even more intriguing, we saw Diana this morning-"

"Tolly's Diana?"

"-yep, and she'd done a painting of Gundry's Tower years ago which showed there were some extremely rare flowers," she paused, hoping he was keeping up with her. "If those flowers are still there-"

"That would be reason enough to halt the work?"

"Exactly."

He got it and, delighted, she paused to catch her breath.

"Sooo," Mike was thinking, "that's a potential turning point. But how can I help with any of that?"

Phoebe breathed deeply. "We can't get hold of anyone. No one at the Council is available and it's nearly the weekend. The work is due to start on Monday-"

"It'll go right down to the wire."

"And I wouldn't put it past them to start doing something over the weekend, thinking it's quiet."

"I see."

"I think we need to get some publicity, make the public aware so it's not just swept under the carpet on Monday."

"Um."

She can hear the questions already forming in his mind. "I wondered how the Wanderers would feel about a protest-"

"A protest?"

"Yes." Phoebe sounded way more confident than she felt. "All of us camping out tonight, maybe over the weekend. We need to make sure nothing happens on site. We could put a post on social media, get in touch with local rambling groups…" she paused, waiting for his reaction, then sighed. "I'm just making this up on the hoof."

"Are you sure? I mean, it sounds great but what about your job? Won't there be ramifications?"

"I've been thinking about that. In my defence, I have tried my hardest to find out what's happening, but I've been blocked, or ignored. If I don't do something about this, what example am I setting to Celeste?"

"You set a great example to Celeste," his voice softened at the other end.

"I'm not sure. I'm teaching her to keep the peace, to stay quiet-"

"You're being really harsh on yourself."

"Well, no one's listening, are they? I've *tried* the proper routes," her voice rose in frustration. "Rita's tried too. We've left messages and got nowhere." She paused and took a deep breath. "We've done all we can on our own."

"Mmm."

She could picture Mike thinking, his eyebrows knitting together while he ran through the options.

"But you're not on your own anymore, are you?" he said slowly, and she smiled. She liked the sound of that.

"If you're *really* sure about this-"

"I am!" She said defiantly, realizing she was about to go past the point of no return.

"Well," he replied calmly, "I'd better make some calls and mobilise the troops then, hadn't I?"

Chapter Twenty-five

A HUSH FELL across the camp as Phoebe walked back to her chair, hand in hand with Celeste. The little girl still wore her school uniform, skipping next to her mother, and Rita paused talking to Tolly when she saw her.

"I've made a call to the Simonton Reporter," Phoebe said. "They'll pass it on to the News desk, probably be tomorrow now, but they've got my details and number."

No one spoke.

"I've explained the work is due to start on Monday and we're going to camp here until then."

Eddie smiled at her. "That sounds promising; hopefully someone will be in touch tomorrow then."

"Great, we need to get as much publicity as possible," agreed Rita. "I wouldn't trust any of these workers not to dig up the ground before then." She rubbed her chin, thinking about something then spoke to Phoebe. "Do you remember that planning at Gerard's Folly?"

Phoebe's eyes widened. "I do; it was awful." She remembered it very well; it had caused controversy across the country and happened not long after she'd started working at the Council. For the benefit of the others, she explained;

"A farmer wanted to demolish a grade two listed folly that sat on the boundary of his land. A popular detour for walkers, he wanted to re-use the space to build a cabin to rent to holiday makers. He was refused planning permission-"

"Good," whispered Tolly.

"-but he demolished it anyway."

A gasp rose from those listening.

"When the Council investigated," Phoebe continued, "he was found to have breached the law and was given a measly fine."

"Good!" Tolly said again.

"It *was* good," Phoebe nodded at him, "however despite the monetary fine, a quirky, old, *beautiful* two storey structure was still gone, forever." Phoebe paused to see the effect her words had on everyone. The Wanderers all looked disgusted, and Phoebe couldn't help but smile at the picture they made, sitting in camping chairs across the entrance to the building compound.

"That is *exactly* why we need to protect the Tower," Rita chimed in, just in case anyone didn't understand the full implications of what was at stake.

"But they're not talking about demolishing the Tower-" Eddie frowned, confused by the comparison.

"The principle is the same though, Eddie," Phoebe said kindly. "If the diggers get in there and rip up the landscape, those flowers could be lost forever." This silenced the campers; their heads now nodding in understanding.

"But what can we do about it?" Tolly sat up straight and Rita waved for Phoebe to explain. She stood up and started to talk through her plan.

"We need to stay here and remain across the entrance so that neither the diggers nor workers can access the land around it."

"But won't that just annoy everyone?" Eddie asked, looking worried and Phoebe shrugged. She no longer believed that someone else would sort it out for them; they were going to have to do that themselves.

"If the Council see the protest and agree to stop the work, then that's great. We'll back off and go home," she said, quite reasonably, relieved to see Rita and Mike nodding in agreement.

"Exactly," said Rita. "We're not out to make trouble-"

Eddie still looked uncertain about the plan.

"-but we must assume they won't get the message in time. No one's returned our calls, and the diggers could roll through on Monday morning. As Phoebe just said, their tyres alone will churn up that site."

Phoebe didn't want that to happen and now she was ready to stand up and be seen. "We've got camping equipment," she looked to Mike. "We could set that up?"

"There's not many of us." Tolly counted the heads of those sitting in a line. "I know, what about Jack? We could ask him and his Duke of Edinburgh friends to come up for support? And they're on that Pinstagram, they might put a message on there-"

Phoebe caught Mike's eye and suppressed a giggle.

"-they'll know how to spread the word, I'm sure."

"That would be great, thank you." Phoebe felt a bubble of excitement beginning to rise. They were finally taking matters into their own hands, and Rita was right; they needed to defend the area until the work was stopped *legally*. She stood and turned to address the Wanderers. "Anyone who is willing and able, can stay."

A low level of chatter broke out as they started to discuss their options. Rita got up.

"Everyone," she raised her voice. "Just remember, we need to stay near here. Don't allow people near the Tower as they could trample the habitat." She looked at Tolly. "That's most important. We need to block the entrance."

Tolly and Mike nodded. They moved away to make a list of any other camping equipment that would be needed.

"Eddie," Phoebe walked over and sat down next to her. "Could you ask Jack if he knows anyone who's good with social media? The more people that know about this the better. They need to do a simple message; explain why we're protesting, as the work threatens to destroy the habitat and could mean the loss of, what we believe to be, very rare flowers. Oh," she clicked her fingers, remembering Rita's warning. "Remember, people should come to the car park if they want to get involved. They mustn't trample around the Tower."

"You're good at this," Eddie narrowed her eyes at her, impressed. "I'll call him and see what he says. Hey, maybe you should work in PR?"

Phoebe batted away the comment but felt her confidence grow a little; she did seem to have found her voice. She clapped her hands for attention. "Right. Who is camping out tonight?" Everyone's hand went up. Even James was persuaded after a nudge in the side from Diana. It seemed that most of them wanted to be part of this. "So how many tents do we have?"

"We'll sort the tents, Phoebe." Mike was standing next to Tolly and, between them, they were making a list. "Leave that to us."

"Do you want us to go to the supermarket for supplies?" Diana asked. "James can drive me?"

After the whirlwind of activity, the site began to empty out. Rita and Phoebe sat together and Phoebe took a breath, curling her toes inside her flat pumps.

"I'm sorry. I shouldn't have just arranged all this on my own. I should have called you first."

Rita shook her head and squeezed Phoebe's hand. "I'm glad you did. I wouldn't have thought to get the Wanderers involved, or to do a protest. I was racking my brains about how to get the Council's attention before Monday. Hopefully this will do the trick."

"I wish I'd spoken up earlier," Phoebe paused. "I was so worried about losing my job."

Rita nodded. "I can imagine. You've got a lot of responsibility. You're only a young girl."

Phoebe scoffed. She raised her eyebrows. "I don't feel it."

Rita patted her hand. "But you are. You're doing an amazing job with that little one." They looked over to where Celeste was now writing the list, as Mike and Tolly named the equipment they needed to collect.

"This is just one hiccup. You've arranged all of this, now stop beating yourself up."

Phoebe nodded. She *had* done the right thing and they couldn't do anymore now, other than continue to put the message out until someone in a position of authority came to speak to them.

"Come on," Rita interrupted her thoughts. "Let's see what happens. You know, I think between us we could be a force to be reckoned with." Rita clenched her fists and pretended to box.

Phoebe laughed. "Grrr." She raised her fists too. She could feel the beginnings of a rebellious streak and it felt good.

Rita stopped jumping around. "Have you ever been arrested?"

"What? No!" Okay, so maybe she didn't feel *that* rebellious.

Rita laughed. "Only kidding. They don't tend to drag people off to the nick like they used to do. Half the cells are closed now anyway, but that's a campaign for another day," she laughed. She got up, waving for Phoebe to join her, and together they went to check on how the camping plans were coming along.

Chapter Twenty-Six

Phoebe sat in her camping chair, cradling a mug of hot coffee. She blew across the top, watching the wisps of steam being moved by her breath. Celeste was to the side of her and to the right, stretching across the cattle grid and the entrance to the Tower, were the Wanderers. All the tents were pitched in a line, blocking off access. Rita and Sadiq were positioned in the middle, ready for any confrontation. It had been a unanimous decision that Phoebe and Celeste should be to the side, Rita insisting, for fear that some rogue digger might try to push through.

"This is more boring than I thought it was going to be." Tolly tapped a foot. He'd already helped Mike put up all the tents and had made coffee or hot chocolate for everyone.

"You'll be able to help me start the supper later," Eddie patted his arm. "Just enjoy the quiet." It was *very* quiet. They hadn't seen anyone since arriving. Phoebe had expected to see at least a handful of ramblers, or a lone dog walker. Nothing.

"I suppose it is Friday evening," Tolly mused, and Eddie frowned at him, not following his logic.

"What's that got to do with anything?"

"Everyone will be out eating or going to the cinema." He seemed to brighten at the thought. "Tomorrow will be busier."

"We did say we fancied a night away," Eddie murmured.

"Um, I was thinking more of a luxurious hotel rather than being back in that thing." He pointed to his tent and Phoebe noticed, not for the first time, that he rubbed his hip whenever he mentioned the tent.

"Hopefully it'll just be for one night-"

"*This* time." He interjected, looking pointedly at Eddie. "I don't know why you don't want to meet Jeff and Steph."

"Because you'll gang up on me," Eddie sulked, and a silence descended between them.

"Is that the same Jeff and Steph who have the motorhome?" Phoebe asked, draining her mug and Eddie groaned. Mike squeezed Phoebe's knee, and he rolled his eyes at her.

"Now you've done it. Don't get Eddie started about a motorhome."

"I think it's a ruddy good idea," Tolly murmured. "We could tour the country in the lap of luxury, now I'm getting older."

Eddie looked at him, her features softening. "It *is* a good idea, I never said that it wasn't. Let's discuss it once we know what our finances are looking like, eh?"

A car approached in the dimming light, headlights on full beam and distracted, Tolly let the motorhome conversation go. A horn sounded several times as it got closer, breaking the peace.

"What's all that noise now?" Tolly tutted, standing up as the car pulled to a halt and parked next to the hedge. A girl was behind the wheel, but Jack hopped out from the passenger seat.

"Alright grandad. Hi everyone, how's it going?"

"There's nothing happening," Phoebe replied honestly. "We've seen no one."

"Oh." Jack's face fell. He looked around as if he didn't believe her, then grabbed a picnic blanket and flapped it open. "You remember Mia, my girlfriend?" The girl joined them, giving everyone a wave before grabbing the corners of the blanket and helping Jack to lie it on the ground.

"We've put a short message out across social media," he said.

"Already had a few likes and shares, so word is getting out," Mia offered as she sank down on the blanket. "Nothing more we can do now, apart from wait."

Mike had brought a fire pit, along with a trailer full of kit. He carried the metal bowl over and set it going, lighting kindling over a wax block. He waited for it to catch then added two logs. As the wood started to burn, it gave off heat and a flickering glow and unable to resist, the Wanderers drew their chairs around in a circle. As the sun set, a relaxed atmosphere settled over the makeshift camp. An air of anticipation hung over them, as if they were waiting for something to happen. But nothing did. They ate their supper, washed up and prepared for bed; they remained the only people around for as far as they could see. Staring into the fire, Celeste yawned; she tried to stifle it but was too late, her mum had spotted her.

"I think this little one needs to go to bed." Phoebe ruffled her hair. Celeste pulled away and smoothed it down, frowning at her mum.

"Not yet, mama. I want to stay up."

"Maybe a few minutes." It wouldn't hurt, Phoebe thought, remembering an earlier conversation with Eddie. She did need to loosen the reins… just a little, but her thoughts were interrupted by Mike yawning loudly.

"Blimey, close your mouth Mike, a digger's coming" Jack shouted, and a ripple ran around the camp.

"Sorry guys. I'm shattered; it's been a busy day."

Tolly nodded. "It has," he agreed, "and as I've already identified, I'm not getting any younger." He stood and gently straightened, before looking at his watch. "I know it's only just gone nine, but I feel like I need some sleep. We don't know what time anything might kick off in the morning."

Phoebe raised her eyebrows at him. "Assuming anything *is* going to happen tomorrow?" She was beginning to wonder if this was going to be a damp squib. There might be no response until Monday.

Tolly shrugged. "Jack? What's the scout motto?"

"Be prepared."

"Exactly. And I'll be better prepared if I've had a good sleep."

"Me too." Celeste jumped up. "I'm ready for bed now." To Phoebe's surprise her little girl disappeared into her tent and, as if that was everyone's cue, one by one the Wanderers settled down for the night.

Chapter Twenty-Seven

"What the-?" Tolly sat up in his sleeping bag. Engines revved outside, and the tent was flooded with light.

Eddie moaned on her camp bed next to him. "What time is it?"

Tolly twisted his wrist to see his watch. "Not yet six. What the ruddy-" He grabbed a jumper and threw it over his tartan pyjamas. He was out in the porch area, his feet in wellies, before you could say 'Troops on parade.' He covered his eyes under the glare of car headlights, waiting for his eyes to adjust. He heard Jack shout behind.

"Grandad. Look." His arm was tugged, and Jack was pointing to the road. It was lit by car headlights; a long snake of them weaving off into the distance. Jack jumped up and down beside him.

"Isn't it great? The whole college must be coming. Some of them have brought their parents, grandparents too by the look of it. There!" Tolly had a phone shoved under his nose, pictures and photos whizzing past as Jack scrolled through. "There's been thousands of likes. Everyone's getting involved."

A van with a satellite dish on its roof pulled into the car park, the other cars parting to make way for it.

"Oh my god, grandad. Southern News are here. That's Angela Oaks. She's coming this way. Oh my god."

Tolly gathered himself. The elegant woman was marching straight towards him. She was fully made up and smiling, her blond hair immaculate; he became acutely aware that he was standing in a field wearing wellies and pyjamas when Mia suddenly appeared at his side.

She was dressed, her hair neat and she smiled at him, excitement written across her face.

"I got this," she whispered and took a step forward, holding her hand out to shake Angela's. Jack sighed and Tolly turned to see him swooning over his girlfriend. He had a glint in his eye as he watched her talking to this Angela-woman.

"She's a confident young lady," Tolly sniffed. He was a little put out that she'd taken over, but then she turned and waved to them. As they approached, however, she held her phone out to Jack and asked him to take some pictures of her with Angela, for their social media campaign. Silently, Tolly stepped to the side and left Mia talking to Angela. He had to admit, Mia was rather engaging. Angela motioned for the camera man to come over and within a couple of minutes they were being recorded as she talked to Mia in front of the Southern News team. It didn't take long. They wrapped up swiftly and as the crew moved away to take shots of the traffic queue, Mia bounded over.

"It'll go out after the lunch time news," she said. "Wow, it's pretty cool, isn't it?" She beamed as she looked around. "I hope you don't mind Mr. Tucker-"

"Colonel," Jack whispered. "Colonel Tucker," he repeated when he saw her frown.

"Sorry, Colonel Tucker."

"Tolly, please." Tolly waved his hand. "Or Jack's grandad, whichever you prefer."

"I didn't mean to butt in, I hope you don't mind. I'm doing media at college and that will be great for my journalism module."

Tolly didn't understand half of what she'd just said but nodded anyway, caught up in her excitement. "Of course, no problem." He was secretly relieved. He didn't mind doing interviews and had represented his regiment several times over the years, but he was still in his pyjamas, he hadn't brushed his teeth or combed his hair yet and there were still standards to maintain even in the middle of a publicity campaign.

"Why don't you go and get dressed," Jack said softly. "Mia and me can hold the fort."

"Mia and I," Tolly corrected before returning to his tent. Eddie's head was poking out the canvas; the opening zipped up to her chin as beady eyes peered around.

"What is going on?"

"Word has got out, that's what is going on."

She moved away from the zip and allowed him access. He paused to zip it up behind him.

"The world's gone bloody mad." He stood in the middle of the tent. He often found himself gazing around, having gone into a room to get something only to forget what he'd gone for. He had that feeling now.

"Clothes!" He suddenly remembered. "We need to get dressed. There's a media storm brewing and we need to be there."

"What do we want?" Rita stood in front of a gathering crowd. She was trying to start a chant.

"The work to stop," Sadiq shouted. He looked round, his face flushing when he realised he was on his own.

"When do we want it?" Rita carried on, undeterred. She stared at him, defying him to stop.

"Now?" Sadiq responded quietly. He held his hands up and Rita rolled her eyes. She waved her hand in a circular motion. She was going again.

"What do we want?" The loud hailer screeched.

"The work to stop." Eddie, Tolly, Celeste and Phoebe joined in.

"When do we want it?"

"Now!" Sadiq punched the air.

"What do we want?"

Tolly could tell from her shout that Rita was smiling. "The work to stop," he yelled.

"When do we want it?"

"Now!"

The chanting was ringing in Phoebe's ears. She didn't know how much longer she could keep going with 'what do we want?' 'When do we want it?'. She looked out across the sea of heads to see if she could see Rita or Sadiq, but there was no sign of either of them. She stopped chanting and motioned for the crowd to stop too. As a hush fell over the field and the impromptu campsite, a flicker of fear passed over her; everyone had turned to look and they were expecting her to speak.

"Um, hi everyone." The megaphone squealed and an 'oooo' rose from the crowd. She twiddled with a button on the top and leaned in. "Is that better?" A cheer rang out and she smiled. Mike stood by the nearest stone gate post watching her, Celeste sat on a blanket to her side. "I just wanted to give everyone's vocal cords a little break," she coughed. "I don't know about you, but I'm starting to feel a little hoarse."

Someone neighed in the audience and a ripple of laughter ran around those closest.

"Thank you," Phoebe gave a little curtsy, her eyes on the teenage funnyman.

"I just wanted to thank you for coming out here today. For showing up and for joining us, the Happy Wanderers," she nodded towards the gang, gathered in a group near Mike. "We couldn't do this without your help and support, and it's made us all the more determined to stay here until someone from the Council comes to talk to us, to explain what is happening." She paused, her mind running over things to say. "Has anyone heard of Gerard's Folly?" A murmur ran around those watching. "It's not around here, but it made the national headlines a few years ago." She grimaced at Mike, but he nodded for her to continue so she took a deep breath. "A farmer wanted to demolish a grade two listed folly that sat on his land. A bit like Gundry's Tower it was a popular place for walkers, but he wanted to build a cabin for holiday makers. When he was refused planning permission-" Phoebe paused, everyone in the field was silent, "he demolished it anyway." There was movement in the crowd, along with a few gasps; someone shouted "no!"

"Oh yes!" She replied, warming to her speech. "He was given a fine for breaking the law, but it was too late for the folly which was lost forever." She paused, allowing the impact of her words to reach those listening. "That is why we are here; today. We *might* find out that those flowers aren't at the Tower anymore," she continued, "but unless we know that for certain, we can't let those vehicles gain access; their tracks will trample and destroy anything in their wake."

In front of her a few people sat down on the floor. She frowned, were they bored with her rhetoric? Then more sat down, taking their places next to each other. Within a few minutes those sitting down had formed a line in front of the gateposts, a line which stretched from one side to the other, and everyone began to interlink their arms.

"That's right," she laughed, "they cannot be allowed to pass. Thank you."

She put the megaphone on the floor and jumped off the bucket, as a cheer rose. Those listening weren't bored at all; they were forming a barricade and, as she pushed her way through to Mike, people patted her on the back.

"How was I?" She asked, breathing heavily.

"Magnificent," Mike kissed her on the cheek. "Listen." They could hear the crowd; were they singing? Quietly at first, Phoebe recognised it as the chant from earlier; the noise getting louder until Phoebe could clearly hear the words.

"What do we want? The work to stop. When do we want it? Now!"

She looked over at the others, a huge grin plastered on her face. They were chanting too, and every time they shouted the word 'now' they raised their fists in defiance.

Tolly lay on his camp bed. He was exhausted. His throat hurt and his voice was now a croak after hours of shouting; he'd been extremely vocal, when not making cups of tea for the Wanderers or standing on the line across the entrance. They now carried on outside without him. He just needed a little forty winks and he'd be back out there with the rest of them. He smiled to himself. He was rather enjoying it. He'd felt a camaraderie and sense of closeness with James and his family that had been missing for quite a while. He chuckled. Phoebe had also come into her own. She'd stood on a bucket at the front, next to Rita, and talking quietly at first, she had ended up with a rousing speech. He nodded in admiration. She was one to watch, a natural public speaker. Gently and with authority she'd appealed to the emotions of the crowd and by the end, they were sitting in peaceful protest. Now no one was getting past the line of bolshie ramblers without the express say-so of the Wanderers.

Chapter Twenty-Eight

AMIR WALKED to the door of the camp shop and held it open for the man and his young son to exit.

"Thank you. I hope you get good use out of it."

The boy hopped with excitement as he clutched a new sleeping bag. Amir had heard all about the Scout Jamboree he was attending in two weeks' time—it sounded as if it was going to be fun. He waved as they headed off down the street, pausing in the doorway to watch. He liked the idea of a camping trip; he'd not been outside these four walls for what felt like an age. He stepped onto the pavement, another beautiful day and already late afternoon. The months were passing him by, the year rolling along at an alarming rate. He looked up and down the High Street and frowned. It was very quiet—even for this time on a Saturday—given that the town had started to get busy with tourists over the last few weeks. He went back indoors and brought up a spreadsheet on his laptop. It showed the date and items sold. He also had a column for cost price and sale price, which then calculated the profit. He typed in details of the sleeping bag and checked that it had pulled the figures through correctly into the other columns. He moved the cursor to hover over the second tab; he felt a flicker of anticipation, like checking a lottery ticket. On screen, a graph appeared. A blue line showed turnover and the second, in green, showed profit. Both were steadily climbing, and he smiled at the progress. He couldn't afford to buy one of the houses in Mike's estate just yet. His smile dropped. Thinking of Mike brought an image of Heather to mind. His eyes lifted from the screen, and he gazed at the door. He needed to go and see her; but if he did, he worried that he'd put his foot in it, say the wrong thing *again*. He was no good with words. Dejected, he looked back at the screen. At least he understood numbers. This upward trajectory was good news at last—the bad news was it was taking too long. The full business rates would kick in soon. He'd had six months grace to establish the business and he didn't know how to speed up the sales. He saved the document and folded away the laptop. He was doing everything right, even opening seven days a week. His life *was* this shop, and what a bitter-sweet relationship it was turning into. He couldn't imagine doing anything else, but he also didn't know how much longer he could do it for. He scoffed; that didn't make sense, but before he could analyse it too much, the phone rang.

"Simonton Camping Supplies. Amir speak-"

"Amir, Amir! It's me. Dad."

Amir recognised the voice which breathed heavily down the phone. "Hi Dad. You okay?"

"Son, I'm calling from Gundry's Tower. You need to come up here. Can you shut the shop?"

"Shut the-? Dad, I can't. What's going on?"

"You know they're planning to build up there?"

"Uh-huh." Amir had been kept up to date by Jack.

"Well, they're holding a protest, blockading the access for the developers. There might be some rare flowers up here. That Phoebe-"

"Mike's girlfriend?" Did Phoebe know about the kiss?

"-she's been trying to get info from the Council; Rita's phoned but nothing. Until someone comes to let them know what's happening the Wanderers are staging a protest. There are hundreds here; shall I come and pick you up?"

Amir sighed. When would people realise that he couldn't just shut the shop? Customers needed him. "Dad, you know I can't do that."

"What? Why?"

"Dad," Amir said with an air of exasperation. "I've got a business to run."

His dad tutted down the line and Amir was transformed back to his ten-year-old self—his dad explaining homework at the kitchen table.

"Think about it Amir." The exact same phrase he'd used then—and it still had the ability to rattle him.

"I can't just close," he protested.

"How many customers have you had today?"

Amir sniffed.

"Amir, this is business. How many?"

"Six-"

"That's because there's nobody *left* in Simonton, they're all up here." His dad paused. "Put a note on the door. Say you have gone to fight for the environment; people will understand. It's a good reason to shut for a few hours."

Amir bit his lower lip. It would be nice to see something other than the inside of the shop.

"Have you got business cards?" his dad asked quietly.

Business cards? "I've got a box of flyers left over from the opening."

"Great," his dad was off again, "bring them. We'll hand them out as we walk around."

It did sound sensible, and he had been thinking about how to promote the shop. Amir felt a rising bubble of excitement.

"Actually," he said, "I've still got some freebies left from the opening-"

"What sort of freebies?"

"Notebooks with the shop's name on, a box of pens-"

His dad grunted, unimpressed.

"I've got Kendal mint cake—those little samples I had printed with the logo?"

"That's better," his dad cheered up. "Bring them. I'll help you give them out. Anything else you can sell?"

"I can't start selling stuff-"

"Why not?" His dad argued. "There are food wagons, and an ice-cream van here already. People might want a blanket to sit on, or a hat or gloves. Maybe those pouches of food if people are staying tonight." His dad paused for breath. "Pack some boxes and we'll fill the boot. Bring one of the shop banners too, and some water carriers, full of water."

Amir leant against the counter, nodding. He was making a mental picture of the items he needed to pack.

"This is going to be like old times, you and me," his dad chuckled. "I'll be outside by four-thirty." The line went dead. Amir looked at the phone and shook his head. His dad's enthusiasm was infectious, and he did make a good argument. There was no point staying here if the whole town had turned out at the Tower; and if he did make any sales, well that would be a bonus. He shoved his laptop further on the shelf—he wouldn't be needing that today—and went to the stockroom to find those boxes.

Amir's dad turned off the main road and onto St. Mary's Lane. Gundry's Tower was just visible over the hill. After a few moments of driving, they rounded the final bend. Sadiq braked, pulling into the middle of the road to avoid the long line of cars parked on the grass verge. They slowed to a crawl and Amir stared out, his mouth dropping open.

"What on earth...where did all these..."

"I told you it was busy."

The car park was full, and people milled around, the sound of excited chatter catching in the air. Several vans were parked in a line selling burgers, the smell of onions wafting through the open car windows. A queue of children snaked away from another van, as they waited patiently to part with pocket money in exchange for a bag of pink candy floss. The place had a carnival atmosphere. Music was coming from the back of the graveled area, where there was a small block of toilets. Amir couldn't believe how it was totally transformed from the haven of peace and tranquility it had been on his last visit.

"We'll never get parked."

"Don't worry, boy. The Wanderers have got it organised." Smiling, his dad pointed through the windscreen to Rita who had appeared, holding hands with Celeste. She beckoned them over.

"There she is. She's a gem that woman."

Something in his tone made Amir look. His dad was leaning on the steering wheel, a soppy smile lifted his mouth and softened his whole face. Amir had a photo in his flat, an old one of his mum and dad on a wedding anniversary. His dad had worn a similar expression then, as he'd gazed lovingly at his wife. It lifted Amir's heart every time he looked at it. His dad talked about Rita a lot and he'd certainly found a new zest for life since meeting her. Amir was truly pleased for him, he deserved to enjoy life again.

"What?" His dad frowned at him. "What are you looking at?"

Amir shook his head and smiled. "Nothing dad, you just look happy."

"I *am* happy." He nodded, suddenly thoughtful, as if just realising it was true. "I am."

"I'm pleased for you. You deserve it." Amir knew it didn't diminish the deep love his parents had shared—his mum would always be part of their story—but it was time for his dad to move on. An image of Heather popped into his mind. What about him? Could he move on? He shook his head; he could only see himself being with Heather, no one else came close.

"Hi there."

Amir jumped, as Rita appeared at the driver's window. She pecked his dad on the cheek and gave Amir a wave.

"We were beginning to wonder where you were, weren't we Celeste?"

The little girl nodded, her curls bouncing up and down as she looked across at Amir.

"We've got a boot full of supplies." Sadiq thumbed towards the back of the car. "Any idea where we can park?"

Rita pointed towards the Tower. "Go towards the entrance, the Wanderers are over there."

"Is Heather here?" Amir tried to keep his voice light.

Rita nodded. "Yep, she's there too. Chatting to her mum, last time I saw her."

Celeste was counting the boxes on the backseat. "There's a space next to me and my mum, on the end." She glanced at the boxes. "Are you going to have a shop?"

Amir nodded.

"Can I help? My mum says I'm good with numbers?"

Amir shrugged, not really listening. He was scanning the crowd to find Heather.

"I'm sure Amir would love your help." His dad nudged his arm and pulled him back to the present.

"I'll show you where my mum is. Come on." Celeste pulled Rita away from the window and they skipped off in front, the car crawling behind as it weaved through the people.

Within a few minutes the shop's banner was blowing in the breeze, advertising Simonton Camping Supplies. Amir, Sadiq and Celeste piled boxes underneath the portable table and, with a navy-blue tablecloth, it began to look more like a market stall than the wallpapering table it really was. Amir laid out drinking bottles, a pile of blankets, hats and gloves; he displayed a small selection of his stock whilst the majority stayed in the car's boot, to replenish if needed. The thought of sales reminded him of his spreadsheet. He lifted a notebook and pen from the box; he'd make a note of anything he sold and add it to his computer later. He bit his lip, hoping it wouldn't mess his system up.

"Hi Amir."

He turned to find Heather watching him; she played absent-mindedly with her side-plait.

"Tolly said you were coming." She smiled weakly. "How are you?"

He pulled himself upright, his face neutral and sniffed. "I'm alright thanks. How are you? Your eye's looking better."

"It's okay." They looked at each other briefly then she broke off to gaze around. "Have you seen how many people are here? It's amazing."

"Yeah, my dad thought I'd be better here than in the shop."

"He's probably right." She pushed a stone around with her trainer. "I can't imagine there are many people left in Simonton."

"No."

Sadiq joined them, bending to shove a cardboard box under the table. He straightened up with a groan, then smiled warmly when he saw who else was there.

"Heather, lovely to see you." He kissed her cheek, then stepped back surveying her face. "Ouch, Amir told me about your accident."

She touched her face. "Yes, don't argue with a pigeon while riding a bike."

"Indeed, it sounded painful. Other than arguing with the wildlife, are you well?"

She nodded, "although," she whispered, "it's a bit weird being back home." She glanced at Amir, "but I can't complain. And work is busy—I'm designing new kitchen sets for Christmas; tea towels, oven gloves, that sort of thing."

Amir glanced at his dad who raised his eyebrows, impressed.

"Good. I'm very pleased you're finding your feet." He started to arrange the items on the table, shooing Amir along as he spread them out.

"I wondered if we could have a chat sometime, Amir?" Heather toyed with her French plait; her hair looked longer, and it suited her. Amir spread his hands out to indicate the table.

"I'm going to be busy here for a while."

She shrugged. "When you get a minute. It would be good to catch up." Her lips twitched into a brief, awkward smile and she stepped back.

"Here they are." His dad pushed a white box along the table towards them. "The Kendall mint cake. Listen, I can unpack and do the table, Amir. Why don't you and Heather hand those out, and take some flyers to advertise the shop?"

"Heather won't want-"

She stepped forwards and held out a hand. "I can help. I've got nothing else to do."

Amir frowned at his dad, "but what if you sell anything?"

"The prices are written down," his dad pointed to the list. "It's not rocket science. We'll make a note of anything, won't we Celeste?"

The little girl nodded; she'd been unloading smaller boxes from the car and turned to grin eagerly at Amir. "I told you; I can add up really well."

His dad nudged the box of mint cake samples and held Amir's stare. "You need to get rid of those." He jerked his head towards the crowds in the car park.

Heather picked up the bag of flyers, an expectant look on her face, and feeling slightly backed into a corner Amir handed over his notebook and pen.

"Write down anything you sell, okay?"

"Yes, boss." His dad saluted, making Celeste giggle.

"I won't be long."

"Take your time. Have a look around," his dad waved him away. "In fact, don't come back until all that mint cake has gone." He turned to Celeste, "right, we're now in charge." He lifted his hand and she high fived him.

Amir groaned. "What am I doing?" He appealed to Heather, who merely rolled her eyes at his reluctance.

"They'll be fine," she said quietly. "Come on." She walked off, clutching a handful of leaflets. Amir felt torn.

"Go on, boy," his dad urged quietly, "you've got work to do."

Grabbing the box, Amir followed her as she approached a group of people.

"Hi folks, lovely day, isn't it? I wondered if you'd heard of Simonton camping supplies, in town?" Blank faces stared back at Heather. "It's a new camping shop, and the owner," she waved towards Amir, "is very knowledgeable if you ever need advice or tips."

Amir raised his hand in a wave, his toes curling with embarrassment as the faces looked at him. Bereft of anything useful to say, he merely grinned from behind Heather. She, on the other hand, looked totally at ease. There was no flicker of nerves or any indication of being ill at ease with being in the spotlight. He was starting to understand why she'd been so good in her sales job.

"Anyway," she handed the leaflet over, "I won't interrupt you any longer, but if you do need supplies, he's running a stall in the corner, by that flag, see?" Their heads turned to where she was pointing. "Oh, nearly forgot, does anyone like Kendall mint cake?" She waved Amir over and took several pieces from his box.

"I'll leave you with these free samples," she smiled, her face exuding calm approachability compared to the rictus grin currently on his face. "You might be glad of that with a cup of tea later," she laughed as she turned to go. "Nice to meet you." She grabbed Amir's arm and walked him in the direction of the car park. "Right," she spoke softly, "that got rid of one leaflet and a few bars of mint cake." She glanced at him. "That okay?"

He nodded.

"This could take a while," she mused. "Are we best together or should we split up?"

He blinked, then realised she was talking about now—here at the Tower—and not referring to their relationship! He took a calming breath.

"We're definitely better together," he said, and he meant it, in more ways than one.

Chapter Twenty-Nine

After an hour of trailing around, Amir suggested they get a drink. Heather had spent the whole time talking, telling people about the shop and persuading them to visit the stall. She must be parched. He offered to get the teas while she sat down and five minutes later, they were together on a large expanse of grass, sipping at hot, milky drinks. Further along a group of teenagers had flopped down too. They chatted animatedly, clearly enjoying a break from their protesting duties. It made Amir more aware of the awkwardness that had descended between himself and Heather.

"You're good at this." He pointed to the box of leaflets. There was a handful left and the free samples were almost gone. "I'm a stuttering wreck compared to you," he admitted. "I just don't know what to say to people; I'm much better with a spreadsheet!" He laughed self-consciously, cradling the cardboard cup. "You're so…"

"Annoying?"

He tutted, "good with people, I was going to say." He stretched his long legs out in front, noticing how dusty his trainers were.

She smiled. "Thanks, I've enjoyed it." She paused, thoughtful. "I miss the interaction with people. It's lonely now, doing what I do."

The people next to them burst out laughing and while they waited for the noise to subside, Amir offered her a mint cake sample. He opened one for himself and popped the whole block in his mouth. As it grew quieter Heather took a deep breath, a thought seemed to have occurred to her. "You know, that's why I wanted to help in the shop."

Amir stopped fiddling with the empty foil wrapper and looked into her blue eyes.

"It wasn't because I thought *you* needed help," she emphasised. "It was purely selfish. I wanted to be around people; to have that interaction." She put a hand on his arm. "I wanted to be around you too."

He shoved the piece of foil in his pocket and swallowed. She'd needed him and he'd pushed her away.

"I must have driven you mad," she glanced up through long eyelashes. "You just wanted to run your business and I kept popping in."

He shook his head sadly. How could they have misread each other's signals so badly?

"I thought it was because the business wasn't doing well; you didn't think I knew how to run it." He moved closer. "I didn't like feeling that I was flagging under the pressure-"

"You weren't flagging—you're like an automaton," she laughed, incredulous. "You are *so* hard working and organised, god-" she glanced across at the group, then quieter, she added, "how many hours did you spend doing spreadsheets and projections? I felt a total fraud next to you; I was winging it, making it up as I went along." She shook her head and turned back to him. "You, on the other hand, knew exactly what to do. You certainly didn't need me… or *want* me," she added quietly.

"Heather, that wasn't it at all." Amir shuffled closer to her, conscious that the people nearby might be listening now they were eating their picnic. "I *had* to be at the shop. It's long hours and six, seven days a week. I had to stay on top of social media, do stock control, banking." He groaned. "I couldn't cope with any distractions."

"Distractions?" Heather's head shot up. "I was your girlfriend, I wanted to help, as did others," she added pointedly. "Your dad thought he was going to play a much bigger part in the shop, and Jack would love to work more."

"I can't afford to pay him at the moment—I'd make even less money."

"Money isn't everything-"

"Speaks someone who's got it-"

"But it's not," Heather exclaimed. "Time is another commodity. I wanted to spend *time* with you. If that meant time *in* the shop, I was still happy with that."

Amir swirled the tea in the cup, chewing his lip while this new information sank in. "I'm sorry, Heather," he mumbled, "I didn't realise." He tipped the last dregs onto the grass and shuffled to face her. He crossed his legs, feeling the protest from his inflexible knees. He took her empty cup and stacked it in his on the grass. He leant over and took her hands, noticing her pink-painted nails. "I thought you were keeping tabs on me." He felt ashamed that he'd thought so badly of her.

She laughed. "It's your business, Amir, and you're doing a good job."

He snorted.

"You are! Everyone knows it takes time to get up and running."

He stroked the back of her hand with his thumb.

"But you're not in this alone. You need to let others help… for their sake-"

"I thought you said it was my business?" A smile played at the edges of his mouth.

"It is. But no man is an island," she raised her eyebrows at him, "or something like that." They both laughed.

"You're daft."

She shrugged.

"I love you." He gasped, surprised by the words which had just escaped his mouth.

"Do you?" Heather whispered, leaning towards him.

He nodded. "I really do. I've missed you so much. Will you come home?" He held her gaze, hardly daring to breathe while he waited for the answer.

"Will things be different? I can't go through it all again."

He nodded vigorously. "They definitely will be different. You can come and talk to the customers as much as you like; I might even let up *a little* on my spreadsheets." He snickered as she raised her eyebrows, disbelieving. "You can help me work out a rota. We'll take a day off together, and get dad to step in or pay Jack-"

"Pay?"

"I know!" He laughed loudly. "I'll part with what little, hard earned cash I have if it means I get to see you."

"Eugh," she pretended to feel queasy. "Don't over-egg it."

They leant their heads together and paused.

"Please Heather," he whispered. "Say you'll come back. I need you."

"Okay, I'll come back."

"Yes!" Amir punched the air and jumped up. He pulled her to her feet and in an open show of affection wrapped his arms around her and kissed her soft, full lips.

"Woo!"

He felt Heather smile as a loud cheer rose up around them. The teenagers had paused eating their picnic to watch the live entertainment unfolding next to them and, chuckling, he waved to their audience.

Chapter Thirty

Phoebe sat in a camping chair. Celeste was heavy on her lap, leaning back with her eyes almost closing.

"Piece of cake and tea?" Eddie appeared at her side with a tray. "Oops, sorry," she whispered when she spotted the little girl. "Didn't realise she was asleep."

"Not really sleeping with all this going on, just conserving some energy."

"Here. This might give you both a boost." She pushed the tray towards them. Neat slices of lemon drizzle cake sat on a plate next to steaming mugs of nice strong tea.

"Thanks Eddie." Phoebe motioned for Celeste to move to her own chair, dropping cake crumbs on the floor as she did. When she was safely out the way Phoebe took a tea.

"That might perk us up a bit, eh?" She smiled at Celeste who grinned back, squidging chewed up cake between her teeth.

Phoebe heard the Police sirens and opened her eyes with a start. She must have dozed off. She jumped up. Celeste wasn't in her chair. Her body spasmed with fear as she looked around, desperately trying to find her daughter.

"She's with Mike, don't worry." Eddie was sitting next to her; she'd been reading and lay the book on her lap. "They went with Tolly to have a look at the stalls in the car park. Celeste wondered if anyone was doing hair braiding."

"Seriously?" Phoebe sat back down. "Any excuse to make money."

Eddie shrugged. "There's a lot of people, so it's a good opportunity." The crowd of people had certainly continued to swell.

"What's going on over there?" Phoebe pointed down the lane to where she could see blue flashing lights. "It's the Police." She got back up. Two Police cars were approaching, either side of a black Jeep. Further along the fencing, Mia and Jack were being interviewed by people with cameras. They were holding hands, Phoebe noticed; their relationship seemed to be moving on by the hour. They smiled at the interviewer; it wasn't the Angela-woman but a man this time. The three of them were lit by huge, bright lights and, as Phoebe looked out to sea, she hoped no ships were getting confused between them and the lighthouse further along the coast. Two huge pick-up trucks with the Carpenter Construction logo branded across all sides were parked up in front of the tents; the company had heard about the protest. This was now getting serious… finally! Her thoughts turned to work and the disciplinary hearing on Tuesday. She wondered whether that would still go ahead, or whether she'd just be instantly dismissed, for bringing the company into disrepute or some other jumped-up charge. She didn't relish the thought of seeing Thomas, but she wasn't going to worry about it anymore. She'd made her bed and now she had to lie in it and face the consequences. The two police cars approached, their lights making her head pulse with their brightness. They pulled up next to the trucks and the back door of the Jeep popped open. Her eyes widened when Jason Turner swung his legs to the side and jumped down. One of the doors of a pick-up truck opened. She did a double take as Thomas Johnson slid coolly out. Had her thoughts about work and the hearing manifested him? Her stomach dropped, anxiety pooling, as Mike appeared next to her. He took her hand, and his smooth, warm fingers curled around hers. They stood silently and watched as three men in suits and wellies gathered, with Thomas and a security guard.

"Don't I recognise him?" Mike nodded at Thomas.

She nodded. "The smarmy one is Thomas. It's interesting that he's arrived in a Carpenter Construction truck. It's almost as if he's had a meeting with them before coming here."

"I should go and knock his block off."

Phoebe laughed, breaking any tension. "How very nineteenth century of you; protecting a lady's honour. Thank you." She pulled him towards her and kissed his cheek before pointing. "The older man over there, grey suit, black wellies? That's Jason, the Chief Exec. He doesn't look happy." She took a deep breath. "This is it. Now or never."

"What? You're going over there?" Mike searched her face.

She nodded; her mouth clamped in a determined fashion. "I started this; I'll finish it. Or, at least, see what's going on and report back."

"Want me to come too?"

"No. Thank you though. You stay here, with Celeste; that's one less thing to worry about. I'll be back as soon as I've finished."

"Sure?"

She kissed his lips, lingering as if they were giving her a charge of courage. "I won't be long." She strode towards the small group. She threaded her way through those on the periphery and headed for Jason Turner.

"Mr. Turner," she shouted. When he turned, she put out her hand. "I'm Phoebe Ellis."

"Ah, Miss. Ellis. Nice to meet you. I gather this is your doing?" He raised his eyebrows as he surveyed the party atmosphere going on around.

Phoebe shrugged. "We couldn't get any response from the Council, we did try. My friend and colleague Rita Rawlings-"

"Yes, Rita."

"She also tried via her contacts, but no one had the courtesy to get back to us." She glanced over at Thomas. His jaw was clenched, he looked furious. "We couldn't risk waiting until Monday, when the diggers are due to start on site-"

Thomas stepped forward to argue and she held up a hand to stop him.

"-in fact, the diggers are here already; that, in itself, is unlawful. They will be causing damage to the environment now and we couldn't allow any further vandalism to take place, so we're blockading them."

Mr Turner nodded. "A wise precaution, in the circumstances."

Phoebe raised her eyebrows, surprised and he smiled at her reaction.

"I've already spoken to Thomas. Until we can go over the paperwork properly on Monday, no work will start here."

Thomas's face was set in a huge scowl, anger seemed to be pulsing out of him.

"How do we know we can trust you?"

Mr Turner started, surprised by her implication. She curled her toes inside her shoes; she didn't like being confrontational, but she'd been getting much better at it over the last couple of days!

"You can trust me, Phoebe." He held her gaze and her toes relaxed a little. "Besides, we have the media here and I'm prepared to make a statement to that effect."

She nodded. That seemed plausible.

"Now do you want to tell them, or shall I?" Jason Turner took hold of a megaphone from the back of the vehicle and handed it to Phoebe. She turned it on and after a few seconds of screeching raised it to her lips.

"Ladies and gentlemen, children and…dogs," she laughed, as a collie barked near her. "Thank you so much for coming out to help save Gundry's Tower." A cheer rose from the crowd and feeling something brush her leg, Phoebe looked down to see Celeste grinning up at her.

"Mr. Turner, the Chief Executive of the Council-"

A boo rose from the crowd and, feeling her cheeks heat up, Phoebe paused. "Now, now, people. Mr. Turner has given up his time today to come and find out exactly what has been happening. Until a full investigation is carried out, Mr. Turner and Carpenter Construction have agreed to halt all work on this site until further notice." A huge cheer went up from the crowd followed by a chant of 'Gundrys! Gundrys! Gundrys!'.

Grinning at each other, Phoebe, Mike and Celeste couldn't help but join in with the shouts. After a few seconds Phoebe raised her hands to dampen the chanting and the noise died down. Looking at Mike, she lifted the megaphone again. "I'd like to say a massive thank you to *all* of you for showing your support. For now, we've got the Tower back. We can continue to enjoy this beautiful countryside and these amazing views which hold so many memories for all of us." A cheer went up.

"What about the surveys?" A female voice shouted out from somewhere in the crowd. "What if permission is waved through?"

Phoebe offered the megaphone to Mr. Turner who reached out. Clearing his throat, he looked at the crowd. "A full investigation will start on Monday, and I'd like Miss. Ellis to be part of that."

Phoebe's mouth dropped open. How would that work with the ongoing disciplinary hearing; did he even know that she was suspended?

"We will have to wait and see what that reveals," he continued, "but I will *personally* ensure that any findings are announced properly, via the local press-"

"-Social media?" Phoebe pointed to Mia and Jack who stood arm in arm beside Tolly.

"And social media," Mr. Turner nodded. "Thank you everybody and I'd ask for your patience as we go forward with this investigation." The crowd applauded as he handed the loud hailer back to the building contractor. He took a step towards Phoebe.

"Thank you, Phoebe." He shook her hand again then glanced at his watch. "Let's carry on at nine o'clock on Monday; I've got a beach barbecue to get to." He glanced at Thomas, keeping his face neutral. "You too please, Thomas. Nine o'clock."

"-but Sir," Phoebe stuttered, "I'm currently suspended from work; I don't have an ID to even get into the building-"

"-what?" He climbed in the black Jeep and leaned out. "For what?" He sighed deeply and waved his hand as if batting away a fly. "Never mind, I don't even want to get into this now. Come to Reception on Monday at nine, and we'll get to the bottom of everything. I'll get my PA to cancel my appointments for the morning. Okay?"

She nodded then watched as he slammed the door. The vehicle slowly made its way through the crowd, leaving Phoebe and Thomas standing facing each other. Her hands tightened on Celeste's shoulders as, out the corner of her eye, she saw that Mike was watching. He was ready to come to her rescue if she signalled, but she didn't need it. She pulled herself up straight and looked Thomas squarely in the eye. This man had a lot to answer for and she looked forward to seeing him trying to wriggle out of it on Monday. Let the battle commence.

"Thomas." She nodded at him. "See you on Monday." She turned on her heel, clutching Celeste's hand, and coolly they walked back towards Mike.

Chapter Thirty-One

Phoebe's legs were leaden, as she tried to keep up with Jason Turner's PA on Monday morning. The events from the weekend had finally caught up with her, and she was exhausted, but instead of being able to rest and recover that evening (which was all she wanted to do) she was due out with Agnes at the BBC event. Phoebe sighed, she couldn't let her neighbour down as she'd been planning tonight for weeks. Phoebe increased her speed to catch the woman up, half skipping down the corridor of the Council building. She wasn't sure how this meeting was going to go, and she needed to keep her wits about her. They stopped outside Phoebe's office.

"He said you were to make a drink and get yourself organized, then come to his office for quarter past." She handed Phoebe her old ID card back, then left her to return to her own office.

"Thanks." Phoebe reached for the door, but it opened from the other side. Dressed in jeans and a sweatshirt, Thomas was backing out without looking, struggling to manoeuvre a large cardboard box around the door frame. She held the door open and waited.

"Thomas," she said coolly.

"Phoebe." He shifted the box and walked away down the corridor, without so much as a backward glance.

"Ignorant prat," she muttered under her breath as she walked into her office.

"I heard that," laughed Penny, her head popping up at the desk divider, as the door swung shut. "You saw our esteemed manager then? Good riddance, that's what I say."

"What?" Phoebe stopped. "Where's he going? He's supposed to be meeting me and the Chief Exec in ten minutes."

"He's gone, Phoeb. Went in to see Jason earlier. He's resigned. Decided to go before he was pushed, no doubt."

"What?" Phoebe hadn't had time for her usual coffee that morning. She'd been in too much of a rush trying to organize a very sleepy Celeste before Agnes had come round to look after her; school holidays were always a nightmare. It was therefore taking her brain much longer to compute this information.

"He's resigned. Immediate effect. That box he was carrying… all his belongings. Now, do you want a coffee?"

Phoebe nodded; she needed one—a strong one! She removed her jacket and booted up her computer. He couldn't resign, surely that was letting him get away with it too easily. As Penny returned and handed her the coffee, it was time to face Jason. She manoeuvred herself back down the corridor, carefully, to avoid spilling the precious caffeine, knocked on his door and let herself in.

"Good morning, Phoebe. Restful day yesterday?" Before she could respond he waved her further into the room. "Come in, come in."

His office was plush. South facing with large windows, the light brown carpet was bathed in pools of light. He stood from behind his wooden, leather topped desk and walked over to the conference table on the other side of the room. It had eight seats positioned around it but could easily accommodate more. He waved her to take one. Scattered across the tabletop were documents and paperwork and a stack of files sat neatly in the middle. Phoebe waited for him to sit; she took a deep breath.

"Mr. Turner, has Thomas left?"

He nodded. "Correct." He leant his elbows on the desk. "He handed in his resignation this morning, which I've accepted pending an investigation. Audit will move in to check for malpractice, and there could be criminal proceedings if we do find anything untoward." He shook his head. "It's a bad business, that's for sure. But, as for you-"

Phoebe felt her insides clench; she'd lain awake most of the night, going over different scenarios as to how this morning might play out. The worst-case scenario seemed about to come true and she steeled herself, ready to be dismissed.

"-I'd like you to work with the Audit team. I know you're supposed to be on leave for a few days—before all this disciplinary nonsense took place—so I'll make sure that your office gives them access to the files. Then once you're back, at the end of the week, I'd like you to shadow them. If it looks like there have been any other dubious decisions it will become a criminal matter." He sat back and shook his head. She noticed the bags beneath his eyes; he'd obviously not slept well either. "For your information, Thomas admitted he'd waved through this decision without all the due diligence, but he was adamant that there were no others." Jason paused. "Let's think positively, until proven otherwise."

Phoebe nodded. She didn't know what to say.

"Is that okay with you? It means that Penny will have to pick up your work for a few weeks, until Audit have done their bit. Meantime, I've discussed with Evelyn, in HR, about replacing Thomas. We'll be going back out to advert immediately," he looked at her and smiled, "and I will expect *you* to apply for the role again."

"Oh."

He rubbed the back of his neck and briefly closed his eyes. When he opened them again, he looked straight at her. "It's a lot to take in, I realise that."

He had no idea how much!

"I just want to say how grateful I am that you stood your ground. That took some courage. Others would have backed down, particularly with Thomas trying to frighten them off."

Phoebe shrugged. "I can't pretend it wasn't terrifying, and I've had a number of sleepless nights this last week."

"I can appreciate that," he nodded solemnly. "It's been a full-on weekend for everyone-"

She nodded vigorously.

"- but hopefully we'll get this sorted soon. We'll put communications out to say that you'll be working with Audit and that Thomas has resigned pending a full investigation."

She nodded once in agreement as a wave of tiredness rolled over her, now she was starting to relax and, as if sensing her weariness, Jason reached for a file and slid it across to her.

"Right, I've had my PA make a note of all the files that Audit need to check over; it includes all the planning permissions granted since Thomas started here. Could you spend the morning with Penny, to locate the paperwork, ready for Audit to start tomorrow." He stood up. "Once that's done, I suggest you go home and get some rest." Following his lead Phoebe stood too, still clutching her mug of coffee. He didn't need to know about her hair appointment or the manicure she'd had booked for ages for this afternoon; their meeting was obviously over.

"Enjoy your days off with your family," he smiled, "and once you're back on Thursday we'll start in earnest."

She nodded and turned to go.

"Oh, and Phoebe?"

She paused by the door, she knew she'd have a lot more questions by Thursday but for now she just wanted to go home and get some sleep before the big night out later.

"HR will write to officially reinstate you and to cancel the disciplinary action. I see your ID badge has been returned to you. Welcome back and I look forward to working with you."

Phoebe walked down the corridor and back to her office; the meeting had gone better than she'd expected, and she had a good feeling about what might happen next.

Chapter Thirty-Two

Phoebe's eyes widened in delight as she stepped over the threshold and into the Grand Ballroom of The Conway Hotel, one of London's finest. The room was lit by four huge crystal chandeliers. Art deco side lights added delicate lighting, casting shadows over the displays of feathers and angular artwork and she stopped, her hand raised to her mouth in awe as she wondered if she'd stepped out onto the set of The Great Gatsby. The décor was gold and black. Round tables filled the room, eight chairs at each. White, pristine tablecloths draped to the floor and set off central golden candlesticks perfectly, place settings and menus interspersed with cutlery and glass table wear. Phoebe had been to a few posh restaurants but nothing on this scale, ever. She squeezed Agnes's arm which was looped through hers.

"Isn't this amazing?" She handed over their invitation to an elegant woman who had sashayed towards them wearing a floor length metallic dress. It looked like she'd been dipped in liquid gold as it skimmed over every inch of her body. Phoebe wondered how she could possibly be wearing any underwear as there were no lines visible at all…

"Would you like to follow me, ladies?" The woman smiled briefly then turned and walked effortlessly away on her vertiginous black heels. Clutching Agnes's arm in hers, Phoebe gently pulled her to follow, hitching the skirt of her red satin dress up so that she didn't trip over. They were led to a table at the front; it was in a prime spot for accessing the steps to the stage. The blonde waited patiently for them to catch up, gesturing to the table where other guests were already seated. They now turned, curious about the new arrivals. One gentleman hopped up to help Agnes to her chair, waiting while she made herself comfortable before smiling a polite note of thanks to the metallic creature.

"Agnes Greystone!" A voice boomed from the opposite side of the table and Phoebe turned to the grey-haired man opposite; his loud voice at odds with his small stature. Agnes's face broke into a huge smile.

"I never did! Davie Green, is that really you?"

He sprang up and came round the table to kiss Agnes on both cheeks. The other guests, and Phoebe, watched with interest; they obviously knew each other from somewhere. Davie Green, Phoebe muttered; she recognised that name from somewhere.

"I know, I know," Davie held her in a hug, chuckling, "the years have not been kind to me." He stepped back to survey his friend. "They've not been kind to me; but you!" He whistled appreciatively, "you've not changed one little bit."

Agnes glanced sideways at Phoebe and rolled her eyes. She lifted her hand to mock-whisper to her. "He always was a right old charmer," she said, then louder "and which of these lovely ladies is Mrs Green?"

Davie stuck his bottom lip out. "None of them. I finally saw the light when Mrs Green number four left me for her gym instructor."

Phoebe caught the eye of the woman opposite. She looked to be in her forties, elegantly dressed in a black and white Charleston style dress, her hair styled in a classy chignon at the nape of her neck. She shook her head good humouredly, a look of affection in her eyes.

"This is the only lady for me now," he shouted, indicating the same woman. "My daughter, Arabella, and her husband Jim."

Agnes waved at them.

"And this is Tom and his wife Cecilia. Tom is the producer on Drop Your Balls… the current remake, that is." Phoebe found it strange that no one batted an eyelid at the name of the gameshow; each time she heard it, she wanted to snigger… and now the pieces fell into place.

Davie Green had been the presenter from the *original* version of the show, Bert's programme from the 80s. No wonder he'd greeted Agnes like she was an old friend—they must've known each other for years. It was such a shame that Bert wasn't here to share in the show's newfound success. The evening must be so bittersweet for her neighbour. But Agnes seemed to be enjoying herself so far, and as the lights dimmed and the band struck up, Phoebe was determined to enjoy her glitzy night!

There were so many faces that Phoebe recognised. They streamed up one by one to collect various awards from the charming host, J.J. Stewart. He was every bit as charismatic as the tabloids suggested, and when Drop Your Balls received a dedicated ten minutes of airtime, Phoebe helped Agnes up to the stage to collect the posthumous award on Bert's behalf. Agnes received a standing ovation, Davie gave a perfect well-thought-out speech to his "friend and collaborator Albert Greystone—better known as Bert to his friends," and there wasn't a dry eye in the whole ballroom as Agnes took the award and held it up whispering "for you, Bert." Swept up in the emotion, J.J. Stewart had kissed them all, including Phoebe, and the band had played the catchy theme tune from the show while they slowly turned to retake their seats. It was all over in the blink of an eye and, as the band continued to play on, the lights came up and J.J. exited the stage to mingle with guests. He made it look so effortless and easy and, touching her cheek, Phoebe thought she'd never wash again. She checked her phone to see the time, and noticed there were several messages from Mike.

"*No rush,*" one said, "*but I'll start to make my way to The Conway to collect you both.*"

"*I'm here,*" read the last one. "*I'll come and find you.*"

How was Mike going to find her? She was about to fire off a reply, but shrugged; she'd do it in a bit. It was gone eleven, and whilst the main event had finished, no one seemed in a rush to leave. Agnes was deep in discussion with Davie, they'd been inseparable all evening and the others had taken to the dancefloor as the band continued to belt out a mix of new and classic tunes. The waiting staff seemed to have disappeared, probably to have a break, so noticing that the bar at the back of the room was still serving, Phoebe opted to go and explore. She put her arm around Agnes's shoulder, and her neighbour immediately looked up.

"You alright, love?"

"Yes, all good," Phoebe waved away the concern.

"Do you want to join us?"

Phoebe pointed to the bar. "In a bit. I'm just going to get more drinks."

Davie made to stand up, but Phoebe motioned for him to stay seated.

"It's fine. I need the ladies, so I'll get them. White wine?" They both nodded and, deciding to get a bottle, she left them and scooted around the edge of the dancefloor. Passing through the door and into the cooler, tiled lobby she squinted trying to find the sign for the toilets.

"Phoebe!"

She spun round at the sound of her name and found herself staring at Mike. A jolt of electricity fired through her as their eyes connected.

"Mike?" Bloody hell, he looked incredible. She was used to seeing him in casual shirts and jeans but now, in a dinner jacket and bowtie, he'd have looked right at home in a James Bond movie. He took her in his arms and kissed her. It did nothing to stop the heat now flaming through her body.

"What are you doing here?" she whispered, adding "you look amazing in that jacket, by the way." She felt him smile as he placed his lips on hers again. He stepped back and took both her hands; expensive-looking gold cufflinks appeared beneath his jacket sleeves and Phoebe sighed—he was the epitome of sophistication. His eyes swept over her.

"Wow, you look pretty perfect yourself, Miss Ellis," he growled, "that red suits you."

Unable to channel his ease she performed a strange curtsy, making him laugh to distract from her flaming cheeks.

"What are you doing here, I thought you were going to wait outside for us?"

"I thought I'd come in and surprise you."

"You certainly did that," she giggled. "How did you get in?"

A group of people were walking towards them, and he moved her to the side of the lobby. At the centre of the group, J.J. Stewart laughed loudly and others in the area turned to watch the celebrities glide past. J.J. glanced around, conscious of the people watching them. He nodded at Phoebe, recognising her from the award earlier, then looked at Mike. His mouth dropped open and he stopped in his tracks.

"Josh? Mate, is that you?" He moved away from the group and came over.

"Oh no." Mike closed his eyes, then was grabbed in a huge bear hug by J.J. For a few seconds they rocked from side to side as J.J. slapped him several times on his back. He held him away and looked him up and down, his eyebrows rising higher and higher as he took him in.

"I. Did. Not. Expect. To. See. You." J.J. came in for another bear hug. "Where've you been?"

"Oh here and there."

"You're looking good, Bro."

How on earth did Mike know J.J. Stewart, Phoebe didn't understand? But J.J. was right. He did look good; she couldn't take her eyes off him. Two glamorous women edged closer behind J.J. Were they batting their eyelashes at Mike? She felt her hackles rise.

Mike waved his arm towards the ballroom. "Been a good night?"

"Yes, I think so," J.J. shrugged at the now assembling crowd. "It was alright, wasn't it?" His entourage nodded their approval and Mike laughed as J.J. blew them kisses.

"Listen, Bro," J.J. stepped closer, "I need to bounce, but let's catch up yeah? I'll get my assistant to call you; be like old times, yeah?"

"Well, not quite like old times, eh?"

J.J. laughed out loud and rolled his eyes. "I hear what you're saying Bro, see you soon yeah?"

They watched as he swept out the foyer and into a waiting black Mercedes. Phoebe turned her attention to Mike, noting the huge grin that was still plastered on his face. He looked at her. "What?" He shrugged.

"How on earth do you know J.J. Stewart?"

"Long story."

"Well, let me go to the ladies first, and then I think you'd better tell me."

Chapter Thirty-Three

MIKE WATCHED while Phoebe refreshed the glasses for Agnes and Davie. Concentrating, she ran her tongue over her freshly painted lips then sank down on the chair next to him.

"I've got a feeling I might need this," she poured wine for herself then waited while Mike took a glug from his pint of beer. It caught in his throat and made him cough.

"Come on then," she started, "I think you've got some explaining to do."

Mike shook his head, a feeling of dread blooming in his stomach; he should have been honest with her from the start. In his defence he had tried to tell her on several occasions but they'd been interrupted each time. He hadn't lied… he'd just not really pursued it, worried about how she might react. He took a deep breath.

"I have tried to tell you on several occasions." He clamped his hands between his knees and stared at the ground, his face serious.

She frowned. "Tell me what? What's going on?"

"Do you remember when Agnes thought she recognised me?"

"Uh-huh."

"I summoned up my courage that evening to tell you… but Celeste came in." He exhaled. "Each time I've tried to explain, we've been interrupted by something else happening… there has been rather a lot going on." He flicked her a look and she nodded in agreement.

"Mike, it's okay. Just tell me, I'm getting worried." She stroked his arm, obviously noticing his anxiety level rising.

"You know J.J. was in a boy band?"

"Of course," Phoebe tutted, *everyone* knew The Tin Boys; they'd been one of *the* most popular boy bands of the '00s.

"I was a member too."

A look of puzzlement flashed across her face. She frowned.

"What, when they started out?" She stared at his face, her eyes sweeping over his hair, his nose, trying to make any connection. Mike shook his head.

"No, I was with them all the way through—six glorious years." He glanced down at the floor and when he lifted his eyes up again, he saw the recognition dawning on her face.

"Josh the drummer? You've changed your name," her eyes opened wide, "your *hair*."

He laughed, feeling awkward as she scrutinised him. "Yep, definitely my hair! My name is Josh though, I started to use my middle name when I decided to make a clean break. I didn't want to stay in the spotlight, I wasn't like J.J. or Paulie." Paulie Michaels had been the bass guitarist who had gone on to other adventures. He now presented a property programme for one of the main TV channels and had developed a sizeable portfolio of properties himself.

"I just wanted to disappear."

Phoebe stroked his styled, short back and sides and his head relaxed towards her.

"Now I know who you are I recognise you, obviously. But without those golden locks…" she tailed off. "Why did you cut it short?" In the days of the band, he'd had long blonde hair. It had been collar length and curled away from his face in a '70s fashion' way. He would not have looked out of place playing with the Carpenters or The Mamas and Papas if he'd been a few decades earlier. Paulie had channelled a George Michael look, with stubble and a crucifix earring, and J.J. was the dangerous one full of brooding stares, with well-developed biceps. Mike had brought the 'flower power' vibe to The Tin Boys.

"Once we split up, I wanted to disappear. I needed to regroup, and with that hairstyle I was instantly recognisable. It was the reason why I bought my house on Highwood Estate; the paps couldn't get me there, and I became a bit of a recluse."

"And now?"

He shrugged. "Now I go pretty much under the radar—and I don't miss it at all." He looked her square in the face, searching for a reaction.

"You don't miss anything?" She wiggled her eyebrows, and he knew she was referring to the articles about the parties and the girls.

"It wasn't all true, you know; most of those reports were for publicity. We were so well managed, a rota every day, there wasn't a lot of time for crazy parties… it's true!" He laughed at her look of disbelief; he loved how she challenged him and didn't just agree with him all the time. He pulled her in for a kiss. "Phoebe," he needed her to hear this and he became serious. "I love my life now and I certainly don't want to relive those days… I'm too old," he joked. "I think part of the reason I'm so happy at the moment is because of you and Celeste." Her big eyes widened; she was so beautiful, he wanted to whisk her away from this place and have her all to himself. Agnes laughed across the table and Phoebe glanced across on the alert, before relaxing again.

"I'm enjoying myself too," she whispered, her attention back on him, "and now I know you're a Tin Boy…"

He nudged her with his shoulder and took her hand. "I don't want anything to change."

"It won't," she said, "although you should have told me earlier." She shrugged, "but then, maybe it would have altered how I felt." She pecked him on his cheek; the contact with her warm skin made his heart beat faster.

"But I know now; thank you for telling me, and we'll need to explain to Agnes at some point, it's probably been driving her crazy." She smiled over at her neighbour then turned back to him and held up a finger. "And I just want to say, for the record, you should be proud of what you achieved with the band, not try to hide it away."

He chewed his lip; she might have a point. He'd always played it down, hiding the truth because of a misplaced sense of awkwardness and embarrassment. He'd worked well with the others on collaborations, writing the lyrics and finding the rhymes while J.J. and Paulie were better at the melodies. He smiled; he was beginning to think that with her by his side he could do anything.

"Shall we dance?"

Well, maybe not that! "You know I was the drummer, right? I can't dance!"

"Oh, come on."

Reluctantly he took her hand, deciding that if it meant keeping Phoebe happy, he'd give it a go.

Chapter Thirty-four

Phoebe slowed down. As she approached the drive into Mike's house, she saw that the gates were open. She pulled through the gap; Mike was sitting on the steps by his front door. He beamed when he spotted her and stood up. She cut the engine and popped her door.

"You okay?" She looked at him, feeling a sudden panic that something was wrong. He pulled her gently from the car and wrapped his arms around her.

"Nothing wrong at all. I was just waiting for you." He landed soft kisses on her lips and, as she giggled, they became more insistent.

"What's got into you?" She pulled away to study his face, but he stepped towards her, closing the gap.

"There's nothing wrong at all," he whispered into her hair and she felt a shiver travel down her spine.

"You're acting weird."

He paused. "I was just excited, waiting for you to arrive."

"Ooo-kkay."

"I just want to be near you, Phoebe. I miss you when we're not together." He stepped back and took her hand. "Come on, dinner's nearly ready."

Agnes was looking after Celeste for the evening—yet *another* rerun of Enola Holmes; Phoebe didn't know how she could stand it, but stand it she did, as she'd practically shooed her from the house earlier. Mike led her round the side of the house and into the kitchen via the garden.

Cooking smells wafted on the warm, evening air and she noticed two places set at the smaller kitchen table. He caught her looking.

"Thought it was cosier in here, than the dining room. Glass of wine?"

She nodded, taking off her thin jacket. She placed it on a sofa, along with her bag. "Lovely. Just a small one though."

"Are you on a curfew?" He uncorked a bottle from the fridge and poured her a drink. She shook her head as he handed it over.

"No curfew. In fact, Agnes is staying in the spare room, so there is no rush back."

Mike tilted his head, intrigued.

"But I will have to drive back at some point-"

"Or I could get you a taxi."

She raised her eyebrows and took a sip, gripping the glass to steady her hand. She was aiming for sophisticated woman of the world but felt more giggling schoolgirl. She swallowed, trying hard to ignore the fact that he was standing so close that she could feel his warmth radiating towards her. She took a deep breath, noting his aftershave, he was freshly shaven.

"Phoebe?" He took a step towards her and wrapped his arms around her waist. "Can I kiss you?"

She smiled, giving a tiny nod. She felt herself being pulled in closer and finally his lips were on hers; they felt good, and she sank towards him with a soft moan. Was the wait nearly over? Were they finally on their own? For weeks she'd wanted to feel him close to her, wanting more than a stolen kiss here or a lingering look there. Something, or someone, had always been in the way. His kiss became more insistent, and she pulled him into her, enjoying the contact. He paused. She opened her eyes. *What now?* Why had he stopped? He stood in front of her then carefully took her glass and placed it on the side.

"Phoebe, tell me if I'm totally out of order, but do you want to go upstairs?"

She nodded and without another word he took her hand and led her to his bedroom.

Phoebe lay next to Mike, her head resting on his chest while she gently stroked his skin. "So, I was wondering-"

"Uh-huh?"

She raised herself up on one elbow. "What do I call you from now on?"

"What do you mean?"

"Well, is your name Mike or Josh?"

He sighed and ran a hand through his hair. "Mike's fine. I've got used to it now."

"What do other people call you?"

"Mike—unless they're from the music industry." He moved his mouth from side to side, considering. "No, mainly Mike. And my business contacts call me Mike."

"And the Wanderers?"

"Definitely Mike. They don't even know about The Tin Boys."

"Why not?" Her voice went up an octave, incredulous that he was able to keep it such a secret.

He shrugged. "It just never came up."

"But you should be proud of yourself and what you've achieved."

He pulled a face; his ability to take all his achievements in his stride, and be so nonchalant, was something she loved about him. Despite all his success he didn't have a shred of ego. She lay back down and put her arm across him, pulling him tight.

After a moment, Mike cleared his throat. "Are you hungry?"

"I'm *really* hungry," she grinned. "I've worked up quite an appetite."

He pulled her on top of him and peppered her face with kisses. It made her laugh; *he* made her laugh.

"Me too. You are quite something, Ms. Ellis.

"You're not too bad, yourself, Mr. Costello…Mike…Josh, whoever you are!" She buried her face in his neck and lay still, enjoying the sensation of being in bed with him after weeks of imagining what it would be like. She kissed his neck, his cheek, across to his ears.

"You'd better stop right there if you want anything to eat in the next hour. Otherwise-" He returned her kisses, making her giggle. "Shall we stay here, or do you want something to eat?"

She rolled away from him and hopped out the bed. "I'll just…" she pointed to the ensuite and wiggled over to the door provocatively.

"Seriously," he shouted after her, "you need to cover up, otherwise we'll never make it downstairs." With a chuckle she closed the door. When she emerged a couple of minutes later, she found his dressing gown lying on the bed but there was no sign of him. She slipped the garment on and made her way downstairs. She ran her finger down the banister as she went, unable to stop herself from grinning. This house, like it's owner, was amazing. Wearing pyjama bottoms and a t-shirt Mike had his back to her as he revived what he'd made for dinner before it had been so hurriedly abandoned. For a few moments, she stood by the door and watched him. She'd been desperate for them to be on their own and as she observed him moving around the kitchen, his face lit by a smile as he stirred the saucepan then slid to the fridge to retrieve grated cheese, a warm feeling settled over her. She wrapped her arms around herself and thanked her lucky stars that she'd caught her shoe in that manhole cover! Here was a man who enjoyed looking after her, making food to nourish her. She liked that—she could get used to it—and she wanted to do the same for him. She fancied him like crazy, but there was something deeper; a bond between the two of them. She could imagine growing old with him, and the realisation made her eyes water, as a ball of emotion welled up inside.

"There you are!" In three strides he was in front of her. He put his arms around her shoulders and looked at her. "Hey, you okay?" He frowned, a tiny flicker, as he narrowed his eyes.

"Never better."

"What's wrong?"

"Nothing," she replied, truthfully. "Nothing at all." She opened her mouth then paused.

"Phoebe? What is it? You're worrying me."

"I think I love you."

"Oh." He stopped, taken aback. "What, just because I'm cooking you dinner?"

She laughed. "Partly," a smile tugged at the corners of her mouth. "But I think I do."

"I'm glad. I love you too," he replied matter of factly, "I really do." He pecked her cheek then led her to the table and sat her down. "In fact," he paused, hands on her shoulders, "as soon as we finish dinner we're going back upstairs and I'm going to show you just how much I love you."

Chapter Thirty-five

"So. This is nice." Jack snuck in between his grandad and Eddie and wrapped his arms around their shoulders. He beamed from ear to ear. "I've really missed this. And now we can walk right to the Tower."

"Yes, at last!" Heather joined them. "Little did we know what was going to happen last time we tried to go there."

"But just think, we've managed to protect it, hopefully for generations to come. Aren't you proud of yourselves?" Eddie asked and Jack nodded; he was very proud indeed. Between them they'd managed to get the right of way reinstated, for the time being at least; the fencing had been taken down and the Council's knuckles had been rapped for allowing slack practices to prevail. Thomas Johnson had gone, and Phoebe was now temporarily in charge of the department, while they waited for the formal recruitment process to complete. They reached a gate and Jack waited for, first, Eddie, and then his grandad to go through. He smiled to himself. It hadn't harmed Mia's reputation either once her social media campaign had gathered momentum. Now sought out by others, she was deferring university for a year, while she set up a side hustle as a media campaign consultant. Jack didn't know how that might affect them, now that they were officially in a relationship, but he was proud of her, and the Wanderers, for achieving so much.

"So, grandad, how's the van going?"

Eddie turned round and tutted theatrically. She shook her head. "It's not a van," she teased, "it's a motorhome. She's called Doris."

Jack and Heather chuckled while Tolly shook his head, humouring her.

"*Doris,*" he said pointedly, "is nearly ready; rations are packed, water and petrol levels topped up. Expected time of departure is Saturday morning at ten hundred hours."

"Wow. I meant whether she was running okay, but you're all packed and off on an adventure…Saturday? That's soon."

"There is no time like the present. The bungalow has been sold, Heather and Amir will keep an eye on the townhouse for us, so we may as well take off."

Jack had heard his grandad chatting over the details with his mum and dad. They would be away for a few months, touring around the coastline in the van, sorry, *Doris*. It sounded really cool, and he hoped to get a few weekends away to visit them. He had his fingers crossed that Mia might come too. They stopped walking as they reached the coastal path. The view was magnificent, and silence descended as they took in their surroundings. The fencing had gone, and the area was open for people to walk through. The Tower was visible on the headland.

"Fabulous." Eddie nodded in satisfaction and Tolly patted her on the back.

"It is. Beautiful."

As they rounded the final corner to the path from the car park, they were joined by the rest of the gang. Mike, Phoebe and Celeste stood together in a huddle. Amir was waiting and joined Heather. He stood by her side and took her hand, nudging into her. Diana and James climbed out of their huge SUV. They popped the boot and collected a cool box, before joining the expanding group. Diana insisted on air kissing everyone, but at least she'd changed out of her paint splattered clothes, so no one minded her getting close now. Sadiq and Rita were the last to arrive; Jack heard them before he saw them, the rhythmic tap of their walking poles heralded their arrival, as they marched in time with each other. Once assembled, Jack nodded at Mike and Amir; they collected bottles of prosecco from the cool box and poured it into paper cups brought especially for the occasion. Diana handed them out and even Celeste was allowed a teeny amount, to join in with the group. Tolly pulled himself up to his full height and cleared his throat.

"Thank you all for coming—again—to help us say farewell to Morris. It is slightly later than we'd originally hoped-" a collective chuckle rang around the group at Tolly's acknowledgement of everything that had happened since their last gathering, "but thanks to everyone's willingness to band together, we've been able to protect this beautiful landscape."

"Hear, hear," Mike shouted but was shushed by Phoebe.

"We can at last walk here and enjoy these surroundings." Tolly continued with a sniff, as emotion threatened to get the better of him. He took a deep breath. "Without further ado, as I know we all want to have a drink and catch up with friends," he smiled around the group, "we can finally allow Morris to rest." He walked to the edge of the footpath and onto a grass verge, edging a little closer to the cliff. Testing for the wind direction first, he tipped the urn upside down and a trail of grey ashes caught on a breeze and floated out to sea. The group watched in silence as the last of the contents emptied. Tolly rejoined the group and swapped the urn for a cup of prosecco. He raised it up and paused before adding, "to Morris. It was a privilege to call you my brother," he swallowed down the ache in his throat and took a long drink from his glass.

"To Morris." Everyone echoed the sentiment, quietly sipping at their drinks.

"And to Gundry's Tower." Tolly raised his cup again.

"And to us," Eddie added, looking around at the smiling faces. "Each and every one of us. We should be very proud of ourselves."

"Hear, hear" Sadiq chimed in and held his cup high. There was silence as everyone took a sip, then laughter, as Celeste took a mouthful, pulled a face and promptly handed hers to her mum.

For the next hour the conversation flowed as they sat on blankets and ate and drank, catching up with each other's news. It was a lovely evening, and so nice to be out in the great outdoors. Amir's phone went off, interrupting the party and he jogged away, out of earshot, to have a quick conversation with the caller.

"Everything alright?" Jack asked as he rejoined the group and sat back down. Amir nodded; he leant in and kissed Heather on the cheek. From behind her back, he caught Jack's eye and put a finger to his lips to shush him. What was he up to?

Jack didn't have to wait too long to find out. The hum of an aircraft disturbed the peace and, with a huff, Tolly put his hand up to shield his eyes.

"What a noisy thing-" he broke off. Jack followed his line of sight. An old biplane was flying across the clear sky, trailing a banner in its wake. One by one conversations stopped, and everyone squinted as the plane buzzed in circles overhead. Amir grinned at Heather, waiting for her to notice it too.

"I think it's for you." Jack nudged her then pointed up and everyone watched as she read the words on the banner.

'*Heather, will you marry me?*'

Her face broke into a huge smile.

"So *will* you marry me?"

She turned to Amir who was now balancing on one knee, holding out a ring box.

"Oh my God, Amir. Do you mean it?"

He laughed. "I really do. I can't promise grand gestures every month, but I want us to be together, forever. Heather Maguire, will you please marry me?"

"Yes," she laughed. "Of course I'll marry you." She launched herself at him and planted her lips on his. "I love you, Amir. And I don't want grand gestures *all* the time," she laughed, "just occasionally."

"Okay, I'll see what I can do." He took the ring and gently pushed it onto her finger while the Wanderers clapped in appreciation.

"Well, this is certainly turning into quite an evening," Mike grinned as he clinked cups with Phoebe and Celeste. "And, of course, bon voyage to you and Eddie too," he added, speaking to Tolly. "We'll miss you over the next few months; our walks won't be the same."

"Hopefully you'll be able to come and meet us, every now and again," Eddie joked. "There's room for a small one in the motorhome or bring tents."

"Sounds fun," said Jack. "The Wanderers on Tour. We'll be like a rock band… that's cool."

"Yes, Jack," Tolly deadpanned. "We'll be just like a rock band," he said as he ruffled his grandson's hair.

Chapter Thirty-Six

Six months later…

Phoebe toyed nervously with her shoulder length blonde curls as she watched Agnes. Mike caught her eye, but she could only shrug. Although she'd known Agnes for years, she was finding it hard to read her body language as she shuffled from room to room. For fifteen minutes now they had wandered slowly around the housekeeper's flat at Mike's house. Agnes had received the full tour; the double bedroom, fitted wardrobes and ensuite bathroom; a light, airy kitchen, all mod cons, and enough room for a small dining table; and a large, quiet living room that had a view out to its own, private courtyard garden.

"Come on Agnes, the suspense is killing us."

Slowly Agnes turned round. Her face didn't betray any emotion.

"You don't think it would work, do you?" Phoebe's face fell. Their plans to live like the Waltons, all of them under one roof and looking out for each other, seemed to be falling at the first hurdle.

"Are you sure you won't need it for a housekeeper?" Agnes looked at Mike and raised her eyebrows, questioning, but Mike stood firm. He shook his head.

"Agnes, I've lived here for nearly five years, and it's been empty all that time." He shrugged. "We've no plans for a housekeeper, have we Phoeb?"

Phoebe shook her head quickly, her fingers remained crossed behind her back. If Agnes agreed to move in it would be the perfect solution;

they would be close to each other but not living together. But Phoebe knew Agnes well enough to know that she wouldn't be told what to do. Agnes had to make up her own mind.

"You're very welcome to live here, if it suits you; but please don't feel under any pressure." Mike glanced at Phoebe. He'd got to know Agnes over the last few months, and when he'd seen the For Sale sign go up outside her house it had been his suggestion to tell her about the apartment.

"But love, you could rent it out for a small fortune. It's a beautiful apartment; it's been done very tastefully."

Mike pulled a face. "We don't want to rent it out to a stranger. If it's not right for you, we'll continue with it empty." He shrugged; the money didn't interest him, but he knew that Phoebe and Celeste would love to be near Agnes. If it made their decision to move in a little easier, then he was all for it! Agnes walked back to the living room and over to the French doors. She looked out at the courtyard.

"You'd be welcome to come into the main garden at any time. You could use the greenhouse too, if you wanted-"

"That would be good, wouldn't it Agnes?" Phoebe chipped in.

"-and the veg plot is not used at all," Mike continued. "It's a shame, it could be a productive space; they're always telling us on the TV to grow our own fruit and veg, aren't they?"

"Uh-huh," Phoebe agreed emphatically, while Agnes continued to stare out at the courtyard. It looked bleak now, but with a few pots and planters Phoebe was confident it could be a pretty, private space.

"The garden was more Bert's domain than mine. He'd have loved it here," Agnes spoke quietly, and Phoebe recognised her conflicted emotions. Agnes had lived in that house for so long with her husband; all those memories and all those years, but she also needed a change now and to make her life a little easier. Phoebe nodded for Mike to leave the room; she wanted a quiet word with Agnes, alone.

"I'll just check the fridge is working properly." Mike disappeared into the hallway and Phoebe heard the kitchen door shut.

"Don't you like it, Agnes?" she whispered. "I'd understand if-"

Agnes turned, her eyes wide and excited. "I can't believe he's offering it to me, for a pittance. It's a beautiful apartment."

"You like it?"

"*Of course* I like it! It's amazing. I just can't believe it," she leant in conspiratorially. "I know you said he had a bit of money, but this place is incredible." She patted Phoebe's arm. "My Bert would be in here like a shot. He'd have that greenhouse full of tomatoes and the veg plot would be bursting. I can almost hear him chuckling up there -" she thumbed up to the sky, "telling me what a jammy mare I am!" She laughed and squeezed Phoebe's arm. "I reckon this place would give some of those ex-colleagues of his at the BBC a run for their money," she chuckled.

"So, why the serious face if you like it so much?"

"I've got to keep him on his toes, haven't I? Don't want him to think he's Lord of the Manor."

Phoebe laughed. "He's not like that," she whispered, "he's probably out there now, worrying that you don't like it. He just wants everyone to be happy." She moved in closer. "He says he wants to fill it with people."

Agnes paused, pulling her chin in. "Oh, love, I'm not sure I could cope with lots of parties anymore; I need my cocoa and a book by ten at night now."

Phoebe wiggled her eyebrows. "I think he meant a couple of little people."

The penny dropped for Agnes. "Children?"

Phoebe nodded; her eyes shining.

"Oh, that's different. I can cope with *that* sort of people; I could be your au pair." Agnes clasped her hands together, lit up with excitement. "I'm so pleased for you, and Celeste. You deserve someone special."

They heard the kitchen door open, and Phoebe put a finger to her lips. "Shush, he's coming back… so," she raised her voice to a normal level, "you'd like to move in?"

"Course I bloody would. Where do I sign?"

Mike popped his head round the door. "Can I come in?" The two women nodded, turning to face him.

"Do we have a verdict?" He looked eagerly at Agnes.

"We do. I'd love to move in, Mike, if you are sure. But I will pay you rent though."

Mike waved his hand.

"I mean it. I've always paid my way. Even when I went to The Ritz with Elizabeth Taylor-"

Phoebe caught Mike's eye.

"-Elizabeth said that Richard—Burton, that is—Richard would pick up the tab, but I insisted. Neither a borrower nor a lender be-"

On seeing Mike's frown, Phoebe cut in, "you'll get used to her pearls of wisdom."

"It's true," Agnes insisted, her beady eyes on Mike. "Don't ask me for money and I won't ask you! Anyway, we paid our share; Bert settled up with Richard the following week." She stopped talking as Phoebe and Mike put their arms around her and pulled her in for a group hug.

"Celeste is going to be so happy," laughed Phoebe, "wait 'til I collect her from Toby's and tell her." They stepped back, breaking the group hug.

"When would you like to move in?"

Agnes's house had sold like the hot cake that the teenage estate agent had promised. She'd begrudgingly had to admit that he'd done a good job, despite looking like he was on work experience. The pressure was now on for her to find somewhere and move out; the young couple buying the property had no chain, so it promised to be an easy exchange.

"End of the month alright? What about you, Phoebe?"

Mike grinned and reached for her hand; he looked like a dog that had two tails.

"I'm slowly moving things in; we're going to finish this weekend, then rent out my place. Shall we say a couple of weeks, then we'll help you move in?"

Phoebe couldn't wait. The next chapter of her life was about to begin, and she'd have all her favourite people around her, ready to share whatever happened next.

THE END

Acknowledgements

My first *thank you* will always be to you, the reader, for being kind enough to pick up my book and to stick with it (hopefully) to the end! I hope you enjoyed it and you still want to continue reading about the adventures of these characters.

Secondly, thank you to the Romantic Novelists Association (RNA) and the feedback I received from their new writers scheme (NWS). Getting honest feedback on a manuscript is always difficult and the NWS is a fantastic way for new authors to achieve that.

I'd also like to say a special thank you to Ahone who was generous enough to read my first book, and then said "yes" when I asked if she'd read the second! She provided sound advice for both and because of her I now know the name for a group of butterflies (a Kaleidoscope—isn't that lovely?) Thank you so much Ahone.

Finally, I couldn't do any of this without the support and encouragement of my family, Bella, Joe and Selene—and a special thank you to Chris for his saint-like patience, his ideas when I get stuck and his feedback (?!) once I've written something.

I'm grateful to you all xx

If you've enjoyed

The Postcard in the Window

and

It started with a shoe

please keep your eyes peeled for

the *third* book in the series

coming soon ☺

Printed in Great Britain
by Amazon